THE
TANGLED WEB

Other books by Elisabeth Rose:

Outback Hero
Stuck
Coming Home
The Right Chord

THE
TANGLED WEB

•

Elisabeth Rose

AVALON BOOKS
NEW YORK

Published by Thomas Bouregy & Co., Inc.
160 Madison Avenue, New York, NY 10016

Library of Congress Cataloging-in-Publication Data

Rose, Elisabeth, 1951–
   The tangled web / by Elisabeth Rose.
      p. cm.
   ISBN 978-0-8034-7764-3 (acid-free paper)
   1. Musicians—Fiction.   I. Title.
   PR9619.4.R64T36 2010
   823'.92—dc22
                                        2009053109

PRINTED IN THE UNITED STATES OF AMERICA
ON ACID-FREE PAPER
BY HADDON CRAFTSMEN, BLOOMSBURG, PENNSYLVANIA

To Colin, Carla, and Nick

My thanks to the Canberra Romance Writers group for the brainstorming session when I had a plot problem. My particular thanks to Tracey O'Hara for her brilliant solution.

Chapter One

"Tess, you're still looking for a housemate, aren't you?"

Ian's hopeful voice pulled her up short as she headed for the rehearsal room door, new car keys in hand, the refreshing salt air and crashing waves of Manly Beach beckoning. She grimaced briefly before turning to face him.

"Yes," she said warily, in case he was having a midlife crisis and bailing out on Glenys. "I'm being very picky." So were her prospective tenants it seemed, because although many had inspected, none had accepted.

"Great!" Ian's constantly worried face split into a huge, rarely seen grin. *Oh, good grief! Was he asking to share with her? Please say no*. They'd last about ten minutes living together, then one of them would be maimed

1

or even possibly die. Ian was nice but far too pedantic for comfort. She should have lied through her teeth.

He surged on. "I need to find somewhere for David Montgomery. He's flying in from L.A. tomorrow at dawn. It's an emergency. The place I had lined up got flooded from a burst pipe and he doesn't like hotels. He's picky too." He smiled ingratiatingly, which was more alarming than the toothy grin. Smiling of any sort didn't really suit Ian. His face wasn't used to it.

But wait! David Montgomery? Newly appointed concert master with the City Symphony, Sydney? Australian but lately of somewhere in America. Supremely talented, so good-looking as to need a health warning. A few years ahead of her at music school eleven years ago; the heartthrob of every female student. Oblivious to them all, totally focused on his career. And himself.

"What are you proposing?" She'd been as besotted as the rest. He'd been as oblivious to her as to the rest. She was less impressionable now. If the man had money he could help her pay off the Diva. Loan repayments trumped all and the silver convertible was worth a sacrifice or two. By necessity.

"A few weeks maybe. He'll want to find his own place as soon as he can so it'll only be until he gets settled. The orchestra's paying his initial costs. First week. What rent are you asking?"

Tess calculated swiftly. Only a few weeks. Delaying a permanent tenancy, if one ever eventuated. "Sorry, rent's too high," was the common excuse, but cost wouldn't be a problem here. Maybe David could be convinced to stay on. Tess added twenty dollars. "Three twenty a week. Fully furnished," she added quickly in case Ian balked.

"No worries. He lands at six fifteen so we should be at your place around nine. That suit?"

"I'll have the kettle on." Tess gave him what her father called her Cheshire cat smile as the orchestral manager wiped a hand across his brow in stagy relief.

David Montgomery clipped his seat belt in the front seat of the Saab. "Thanks for meeting me," he said as the orchestral manager closed the driver's door and started the engine.

"All part of the service." The slightly built, balding man concentrated on backing out of the tight parking space with pursed lips and fussy efficiency.

David yawned so widely his eyes watered. "Sorry. That flight was murder. I didn't sleep at all. I think it's bedtime for me."

"It'd be better to stay awake if you can, so's to get into the new time routine as fast as possible."

"Mmm. If I can." He yawned again. The day was shaping up to be warm. When they emerged from the parking station, bright morning sunlight bounced off the glass and steel of the surrounding buildings. "Where am I staying?" They were on a clogged freeway heading toward the city center in the tail end of the morning rush. He didn't recognize the road but he hadn't been in Sydney for quite a few years and things had changed. His

interview had been through videoconferencing. His ré-
sumé and references spoke for themselves.

"In Balmoral. Unfortunately there's been a change
of plans. I'd booked an apartment as you requested in
the inner city area but there was an accident, burst water
main." He smiled apologetically. David's already exhausted body drooped lower in the seat. "One of our
orchestra members stepped in to the rescue. She's been
looking for a housemate so it's not inconvenient for her
and you can stay as long as you like."

Irritation forced David's teeth to clench and grate
against one another. He kept his gaze firmly out the window so the orchestral manager wouldn't see the rising
anger. He burbled on. David barely listened. His tired
brain still thrummed from the roar of jet engines, his
eyes and throat struggled with the aftereffects of air-
conditioning, and the last thing he wanted was to share
a house with some woman who was doing him a favor,
even if Balmoral was an upmarket harborside suburb.
She'd fuss and chatter and want to look after him. He'd
had enough of women for the time being and he never
shared living quarters with anyone. Ever.

"You could have booked a hotel room," he said
tersely, breaking into the flow of words.

"I thought you didn't like hotels." Another flashing
smile. Odd the way the man's smiles looked as though
they hurt. Unnatural. "Just trying to make you comfortable."

David grunted. He didn't like hotels but a night or

two wouldn't matter. At the moment all he wanted was a hot shower and a clean bed. And privacy.

"Tess' place is big. You'll hardly know she's there," Ian said with a hopeful intonation. "It's her family home. She inherited it when her father passed away several years ago. Has a lovely garden and harbor views."

"Tess who?" May as well spend at least one night. He didn't have the energy to go room hunting today. Harbor views? Where were his sunglasses? The glare was killing his eyes. He patted his jacket pockets hopefully. Must be in the bag in the back. Ugh!

"Fuller. She's our Principal Viola."

David frowned. His fuddled brain vaguely recognized the name. Tess Fuller, viola. He closed his eyes to think better. Tess. Of the D'Urbervilles? Hardly. A Balmoral milkmaid. His brain was fried.

The car slowed and dipped downhill. His eyes opened. They were in a tunnel with a very steep descent and harsh white light. "Where are we?"

"The Harbor Tunnel."

"I didn't know there was one." He closed his eyes again. The next time they opened the car had stopped completely. He yawned. "Sorry. I must have dozed off," he said.

"Yes. This is the house." Ian indicated to the left.

A green forest was his first impression, then through the shrubs and trees lining the front fence glimmered a sandstone wall and a white porch with a dark green roof. Old. Secluded. Private. Very classy. A desirable address.

He straightened in the seat and unclipped his seat belt. Ian was already out and removing his large suitcase from the boot, grunting with the effort. David collected his violin and small holdall.

The little gate swung open onto a slate path that led in a gentle curve to the front steps between red azaleas, daffodils, and other flowering things he couldn't name but which had a strong perfume. Ian struggled behind him bouncing the case over the unevenness in the paving. Ornamental white-painted wrought ironwork framed the archway over the porch. David lifted weary legs up the three worn sandstone steps. The holdall hung heavy from his left shoulder, the violin case weighed down his right arm. Please don't let her be a chattering nuisance; his brain couldn't take it. Signs were promising that someone elegant, poised, calm, and sophisticated belonged here.

Ian stuck out a long pale finger and a bell shrilled somewhere. Stained-glass panels down each side of the white door shone red and blue in the fresh morning light.

"Coming," called a melodious female voice and the door was suddenly flung wide open. A small brown-and-white dog shot between their legs and disappeared down the steps. "Fidelio, come here!" she yelled.

David's head jerked back in shock at the volume and pitch of such a close encounter. A brief impression of predominantly blond shaggy hair and wide smile seared his retinas, followed by a flash of white shirt and tanned legs in shorts as she darted past. Some light, fresh perfume tangoed in his nostrils.

Two steps down she stopped and turned. The T-shirt featured a large tiger face. He stared. Brain wouldn't function. Disconcerting, the hallucinogenic image of two sets of eyes, two faces, one on top of the other. "Sorry, go on in," she said in a more human voice. "I'll have to catch Fid."

Ian gestured with an impassive expression and David stepped inside. The wide hall floor was stunning. Beautiful polished timber boards glowed golden around a gorgeous blue patterned Persian runner at least twenty feet long. Immediately on the left through a wide archway was an elegantly furnished living room, all creams and pale grays with a large Australian landscape featured on the wall and smaller sketches grouped beside it. Originals?

No time to examine more closely. Ian led the way along the passage past several closed doors to a big room at the rear of the house. An open kitchen separated from the living space by a black granite-topped bench lay to the right. A large table and chairs filled one end of the area and comfortable-looking wicker armchairs grouped cozily around a magazine table and a TV at the other. Open French doors led onto a paved terrace bathed in morning sunlight. A perfectly manicured lawn stretched away toward trees on the rear fenceline beyond which sparkled an expanse of blue ocean. An oasis of calm.

An indefinable odor hung in the room. Something off in the fridge? The garbage need emptying?

"It's a beautiful house," said Ian. "Tess' father was an investment banker."

David nodded. Money and plenty of it. His own father was a mechanic. A very good mechanic with his own business in the country town of Cootamundra. He'd scrimped and saved to pay for violin lessons for his son and no one had been prouder when David was accepted to the School of Music in Canberra.

The front door slammed. The scraping of claws and paws on polished floor mingled with Tess' voice saying, "Bad boy. You know you'll be squashed on the road if you do that. And keep right away from Mrs. Screech or she'll have you arrested again."

If there was anything he disliked more than sharing a house, it was noisy women and dogs *in* the house.

"Sorry about that." Clear blue eyes twinkled cheerily from under wispy blond bangs. The rest of her hair was a muddle of colors and lengths he saw now—dark brown strands, honey gold, chestnut, and blond all in a riotous wavy mess. She stuck out a slim tanned hand. It had a large opal ring on one finger and the short trimmed nails were bright purple. "Hello, David, I'm Tess. You probably don't remember me. I was at music school with you. Well, not with you exactly, two years below. I had the most tremendous crush on you. All the girls did. Did you know?" Clutching her hand, David was speechless. Even without jet lag he couldn't have countered this flood of . . . of . . . whatever it was.

She turned to Ian with a grin. Hers was natural; his

looked strained. She didn't wait for a response. "He never took any notice of any of us. Broken hearts all over the place." Her blue searchlights swung back to David. Silver earrings dangled wildly amid the longer, thicker strands of hair. Like a lion's mane.

"Sorry," he managed. "I'm a bit . . ." He grimaced helplessly. Could he escape from this loud and insensitive lunatic? Too rude to leave immediately? What was that pong? Rotten potatoes?

"David's completely zonked, Tess. He needs sleep," said Ian firmly.

Her smile faded to concerned dismay. "Of course, sorry. Those overnight flights are hell. I've put you in the Lavender Room." She darted past them both and opened a door that, instead of revealing a room, opened onto another short passageway. "It's nice and quiet, overlooking the back garden. You can shut yourself right away in here."

Lavender Room? Was he dreaming of English country estates? Still on the plane? No. This was real. That pesky little terrier was sniffing at his ankles. He resisted the urge to push it away. With the toe of his shoe. Hard.

"This is your bathroom. No ensuite I'm afraid." She pulled a sorry face as she opened a door on a full-size bathroom complete with toilet, frosted glass shower stall, large white tub, and vanity unit. It had polished wood trim, cream painted walls, white tiles with a black geometric feature pattern. A suspended potted fern draped graceful fronds in one corner. Rose-colored towels hung from gleaming silver railings—heated ones, he'd bet. "But your bedroom is right next door so it's almost as good," she said with another big grin as she opened the door.

Ian dragged his suitcase in and left it by the king-size bed. "I'll leave you to get acquainted and settle in." He backed out hastily. He must have correctly interpreted David's instinctive reaction to the woman, not to mention the dog. Or he felt exactly the same.

"Thanks very much, Ian. I'll call you tomorrow." David tore his eyes away from the bedroom, which, to his amazed mind looked like it was straight out of *Home Beautiful*, or an article entitled "How the Other Half Lives." It certainly was nothing like he'd ever lived.

"I'll see you out." Tess disappeared with Ian. The dog pattered after them.

David stood and stared. The room, for starters, was enormous. In a bow window affair two cream-colored easy chairs faced a coffee table on which sat a vase with flowers. Daffodils. She'd picked flowers. Sweetly welcoming. He smiled and shook his head in astonishment. The bed was enormous and covered in a deep purple quilt with, of course, matching pillowcases. Built-in closets ran along one wall and a large, old-fashioned oak dressing table with an oval swing mirror sat solidly opposite the foot of the bed.

High ceilinged like the rest of the house with fancy fruit and flower designs in the white plaster. It was the Lavender Room because of the pale lavender paint.

Soothing. Cream curtains and trim. Tasteful and elegant. No smell in here save for daffodils.

He was still holding his violin and holdall. He dropped the bag on the floor, took his violin to the coffee table, and laid it gently on the polished surface. Out the jutting bow window a restful expanse of that emerald green lawn stretched down a gentle slope to a stand of trees through which he could just see blue water. To the right the lawn curved around a rose bed and ornamental birdbath before the solid old sandstone house wall blocked his view. Another building was nestled in the trees. The garage? To the left was a path presumably leading toward the terrace and that spectacular view. Everywhere trees and shrubs crowded in orderly profusion, overhanging the path, the garden, and obscuring the fenceline. A picture of sunlit loveliness.

David turned from the peaceful scene to lay his case down flat. He unlocked and unzipped the lid and looked for toiletries, clean underwear, and clothes. That shower was calling. And the bed. One night here wouldn't be too bad. Maybe two. A chance to regroup. If she kept that dog out of his way. And kept her voice down. Was she living in this enormous house alone?

Tess closed the front door behind Ian and leaned against it with a sigh. Thought she was more mature now, did she? If that were true, how come the sight of David Montgomery sent her whirling and spinning back to those student days when she had absolutely adored him? He was even more adorable now, completely and utterly irresistible. Still unattached somehow. Why would that be? He had charisma oozing everywhere. He wasn't gay—everyone would have known that back at music school. No one hid their sexual proclivities there. No one cared.

He was still aloof, though. Aloof and distant. That aspect hadn't changed. But he'd just stepped off a long-haul flight and they were the pits. He wasn't firing on all cylinders. He'd need a shower and a change of clothes and a nice hot cup of tea. Mustn't let him sleep though or he'd be completely out of whack. His days and nights would be upside down.

Tess launched herself down the passageway to his room, wrinkling her nose as she passed through the family room. No sign of Hannibal. Must be outside. She tapped on the partly open door. David was squatting down pulling clothes from his suitcase and looked up with a rather bleary gaze.

"David, would you like something to eat? The kettle's on for tea when you're ready. Or I can make coffee if you'd prefer. Or maybe you don't want a hot drink. Juice? I only have apple juice. Don't like orange juice much. Unless it's mixed with something at a party." She grinned then saw the expression on his face. Kind of stunned. Did he understand her at all? As a student he'd never partied or went to any of the usual hangouts.

He blinked. His eyes widened and he blinked again, shook his head as if to clear his thoughts. He smiled suddenly and her knees sagged. Charisma overload. He still had it. Bags of it. "Thanks. A cup of tea would be great. A proper one? No tea bags?"

"What are tea bags?" she managed to retort as she reeled under the onslaught of white teeth and crinkly, smiling eyes. Chocolatey brown eyes. A maturely assessing gaze. A man, not a boy anymore. Far more dangerous.

"I desperately need a shower first. Thanks, Tess." His eyes caressed her and she almost purred. Then Fid darted into the room, stumpy tail wagging frantically and David's expression turned to fire and brimstone in an instant.

"Fid. Out!" she shrieked. Fid slammed on the brakes and cowered. He turned and skulked toward her. A total penitent. "Sorry," she said to David whose face now resembled a man who'd received an electric shock. He'd gone quite pale. "Fid gets excited when we have company."

"Oh," was all he said.

Tess backed from the room, flicking her fingers at Fid frantically. He, for once, behaved himself and followed just like an obedient dog. She pulled the door closed gently. Maybe David wasn't a dog person. More likely he was tired and disoriented after the fourteen-hour flight. She looked down at Fid as he trotted beside her to the kitchen.

"Don't worry, he'll love you like I do soon enough. Just don't crowd him. Understand? He's tired." Fid looked up and waggled his rear end. He understood. He jumped up and licked her fingers to prove it. "And we don't want to scare him off," she added quietly as she flicked the switch on the electric jug, "because we need his rent money." He'd hardly notice Hannibal, the poor old darling. With any luck.

When David, clean and marginally refreshed, opened the door leading from his wing of the house to the living area with a tentative exploratory sniff, the nasty smell had faded. Two days he'd give it, he'd decided in the shower. Tess was just bearable and the accommodation absolutely and luxuriously beautiful. As long as she kept to herself and the dog stayed away from him.

He discovered Tess sitting on the terrace at an outdoor table set with breakfast and tea things. She'd raised a large canvas shade umbrella. The dog sat beside her twitching and fidgeting. It stood up when he stepped outside but she hissed and it sat down again. She smiled and gestured to one of the curved wooden chairs. "I wasn't sure if you were hungry so I put a few things out just in case."

David sat down in front of a plate with cutlery and a salmon-colored linen napkin placed neatly on top of it. A pile of warm croissants in a basket wafted a temptingly fresh bakery smell into his nostrils. Two kinds of jam were spooned invitingly into little glass serving dishes. A platter of fresh fruit—sliced rockmelon, grapes, strawberries, pineapple pieces, mango. His mouth watered.

Tess poured tea through a silver strainer into the two

big china teacups. Breakfast-size. Milk and sugar waited in a small jug and bowl. All from a matching service, as were the plates. She'd either gone all out to impress or this style was natural for her.

"This is wonderful. Thank you." He added milk to the cup she handed him. A bird began twittering in a tree nearby. Sunlight filtered by the green canopy fell in dappled patterns on the lawn. Warm air wafted gently across his cheek.

"Going to be hot again today." Tess seemed to be on her best behavior now. Lady of the Manor.

"Feels like it." He sipped the tea. Delicious. He helped himself to a warm croissant, split it, and added apricot jam. Hungry suddenly, he wolfed it down and took a second. "It's very kind of you to let me stay."

"Not really." Tess speared a slice of pineapple and ate it from the fork, running her tongue around her mouth to catch the juice. Lady of the Manor disintegrated into something out of an adult movie. David watched, mesmerized. She had delectable lips. He blinked, realized he was staring. Her T-shirt tiger glared at him.

"I think so," he said.

"Not if you're paying rent."

"Am I?" he asked, startled.

"Yes, didn't Ian explain I want a housemate?" She sat up straight, frowning in annoyance. "I don't *want* to share but I need the rent money."

"I can imagine," he murmured. How tactful she was. And refreshingly honest. Blunt. He hated pussyfooting around. She wouldn't know the meaning of the term. Nice to know where they stood. This could have become very awkward, not to mention embarrassing. Had Ian said anything about rent? He'd understood the orchestra was picking up the tab for the first week.

"I own the house," she said in an offhand way. "It's not that. I have car payments to make."

He remembered suddenly. "Oh yes, Ian told me. This is the family home." He swallowed more croissant. Not that he wanted to share with her or anyone else but out of interest, because he'd be looking for somewhere himself, he asked, "What rent are you asking?"

"Three twenty per week. I can't believe Ian didn't tell you!"

"He may well have. I think he did. I don't know." He shook his head. "I'm not functioning too brilliantly at the moment." He drank more tea, considering her answer. Well below what he'd have to pay for a small two-bedroom unit with no garden and nothing like the furnishings or surrounds. "I have to tell you, Tess. I don't want a housemate either. I don't like sharing. And I don't like dogs."

He put his cup down and studied her while she studied him with her bare arms folded across the tiger. "So that's that. You're my guest. How long do you want to stay? I really need to get someone in here permanently." She huffed out an annoyed puff of air.

"I understand." He picked up a grape and popped it into his mouth. Sweet and juicy. Another. And another.

"It's not easy to find someone. I thought it would be but I'm choosy. Or maybe it's them." She shrugged. "Can't have just anyone in here. There's some valuable artwork and stuff plus the music aspect. Practice and so on. Weird times. You know? Late nights, late mornings. I thought someone from the orchestra night be interested but no one is. It's perfect for another muso. I have a separate music studio. I'll show you after, if you like. You might change your mind." She waited, those blue searchlights focused on his face.

He'd never find a place like this for that rent. His room had the little private passageway and the door to the living area closing off the rest of the house. She couldn't be completely impossible to live with. The place was so huge they need hardly see each other. If she drove him nuts or he inadvertently strangled that dog they could call it quits. "What if I stay a week for starters? You'll get your rent from Ian and then we'll see. Depends what I can find. I'll start looking this weekend." Nice. Vague, noncommittal but polite.

She sighed. "Better than nothing I guess. Fine. Deal."

He held out his hand and she shook it firmly and smiled. Exactly like the Cheshire cat.

"More tea?" She picked up the teapot. The dog wandered off into the garden.

"Thanks." He pushed his cup toward her. "How long have you been with the City?"

"Three years. I was made Principal Viola last year."

He nodded. Drank. "So we were in Canberra together,

were we?" He glanced across, surprised to catch the hint of a flush on her cheeks. Besotted with him. All the girls? How did he miss that? Too busy, too worried about doing well. None had taken his fancy, anyway. Women were still more of a distraction than a necessity in his life. Especially after the Marianne experience.

"Yes." Surprisingly succinct coming from her.

He wrinkled his brow, trying to remember her. Tess Fuller. "Did you play viola then or violin?"

"I went in as violin and came out viola." That smile again, daring him to make one of the standard orchestral jokes about viola players.

How do you keep your violin from getting stolen? Put it in a viola case.

What do a viola and a lawsuit have in common? Everyone is happy when the case is closed.

He didn't. He was the new concert master, he wouldn't sling off at his Principal Violist. Plus she was his landlady, albeit temporary. "I'm sorry I don't remember you. What year were you?"

"Two years behind you. I'm not surprised you don't remember me. I didn't spend a lot of time there apart from necessity." The smile dazzled him again. "I had a pretty good time, though."

Something clicked. "You were the Party Girl."

Tess raised her eyebrows. "Who called me that?"

"I did."

"So you do remember me!"

"Only because you and—who was it? Red-haired

girl, pianist—had that wild party at the end of one se-
mester, in my honors year, and the police were called to
your house. It was the talk of the school for weeks." He
stared at her, trying to assimilate the self-assured woman
before him with the vague image of a wild blond-haired
hell-raiser from the past. The one from the very wealthy
family. He remembered that much.

"Vanessa. It was her birthday. A pedantic neighbor
complained about the noise and the cars in the street. He
was a real pain, complained about everything. Not just
about us, other neighbors as well. Dogs, cars, children—
you name it. He particularly hated it when we practiced."
She didn't elaborate further but her smile disappeared.

"I didn't do anything remotely wild. I was there to
work." The antics of the Party Girl were the stuff of
gossip on campus but he was always on the fringe, an
observer. Hearing and seeing but not involved.

"So was I! Those stories are so exaggerated. People
love to gossip and if the facts aren't exciting enough they
invent stuff," she cried full of indignation. "But you
were a total nerd back then. You were extremely frustrating. The best-looking guy in school but you never
came to any parties."

He hadn't made many friends there. Acquaintances,
yes; close friends, no. She thought he was the best-
looking guy? Way back then? He didn't think the Party
Girl even noticed him. But she had scads of admirers
and anything in pants would have been given the once
over.

"I had a part-time job. Two, actually. I didn't have time to muck around."

"I did honors too and I didn't get to be Principal Viola by mucking around." An unexpected hint of steel.

"No, of course not."

She smoldered opposite him for a few more minutes. "Do you want to share food and meals," she asked eventually. "Or keep everything separate?" The look she gave him implied she thought he may want to keep to his nonsocial agenda and avoid her as much as possible.

"What do you prefer?" he asked. No point upsetting her. They'd be working together come Monday. He could be sociable for a week. Especially if this was a sample of her taste and style in dining.

Her eyes narrowed. "Can you cook?"

"Yes. I'm rather good."

The smile flashed on again, brilliant as a fluorescent bulb. "Let's share."

"All right. I cook, you clean up, and vice versa. We share shopping and cleaning." He held out his hand and she grasped it firmly.

"I thought you didn't share. You sound very experienced."

"I didn't say I hadn't shared, I said I don't like to. I'm basing that preference on experience." Her palm was smooth and warm in his.

"Neither do I and so am I." He released his hold. She let his fingers slide though hers. "By the way—I have a cleaner. She comes on Thursdays."

"Fine. We should manage to survive a week if we keep out of each other's way," he said mildly.

"That's going to be hard seeing as we're in the same band," she pointed out. "Will you need a ride to work?"

"I suppose I will. If that's all right with you."

"The first week's on me but share petrol money if you decide to stay longer?"

"Certainly. I'm no freeloader, Fuller."

She grinned. "I'll make sure of that." Her smile was lovely. How had he missed that? The same way he'd missed many other things as a student.

A week wasn't long. He'd start flat hunting tomorrow so he could send for his gear. Without somewhere of his own he'd be up for storage on top of what he'd already paid. Tess was harmless. Quite attractive. That smile could become addictive. She must have calmed down since her student days to be in the position of Principal Viola.

"Coming to rehearsal this afternoon?" she asked.

"No. Ian said they weren't expecting me until Monday."

She nodded. "I'll show you the house. There's an alarm system so you'll need the code. There are three doors and the windows to lock up before we go out."

"And I'll need a key."

She frowned. "I'll get one cut this afternoon."

David stared in astonishment. "You mean you only have one key to this place? What if you lock yourself out?"

Tess fiddled with her empty teacup, turning it round and round on the saucer. "My brother has one but he lives in Melbourne. The security company has one so I call them when that happens. Or the cleaner." She was kidding, of course.

"Does it happen often?"

"Now and again." She grimaced guiltily. She wasn't kidding.

"Why not get a couple of spares cut?" he suggested. "Then you can put one in your handbag as a backup." He'd had four keys to his San Diego apartment. One on his key ring, one with a neighbor, one in the wall safe, one with his cleaning lady.

She said defensively, "I keep forgetting to do it, that's the trouble. It's not something I think of when I'm out and about."

"Had it occurred to you that your new housemate might want a key?"

Her cheeks had turned pink and she looked everywhere but at his face. "Yes, of course, but I hadn't found anyone, had I? I was going to. Now I will."

"What happened to the other keys? There must have been more originally."

Now she glared at him, her voice rose unsteadily and she sat up with her back ramrod straight. "They were lost when Daddy died. He was in a plane crash." To his alarm her eyes filled with tears.

"I'm sorry." What else could he say? His mind groped

unsuccessfully for something soothing and appropriate to say but she didn't seem to need more from him.

She collapsed against the back of her chair, swiped a hand across her face, and sniffed. "Thanks." A watery smile. "It's years ago now and I still miss him."

David tried to imagine how much he would miss his own parents when they died. Immeasurably. They just kept on with their quiet lives, keeping tabs on the four sons and two grandchildren scattered over the country and the world. He'd have to squeeze in a trip to Coota sometime soon. Must phone today, tell them he'd arrived safely. What sort of family did Tess have?

"Are there only the two of you—you and your brother?" Where was her mother?

"Yes. Stuart is very cluey with money. Our inheritance is all invested and he runs that. I have to live off my earnings. Daddy always said we had to be self-sufficient. He put the house in my name years before he died, though." She frowned. "I've always thought that was odd."

"Probably did it for tax reasons. Did Stuart mind you getting this house?"

"No, he got the other places. Melbourne and New York. I don't need more than one home, do I? Stu travels a lot so it makes sense for him to have the apartments. I think Stuart and Daddy figured out some scheme to minimize taxes. I don't understand any of that. That's why I leave important money stuff to Stu. Actually, he insists because he says I'm hopeless."

David smiled absently at her. She was talking about the sort of money he could only dream about. Like this house. She mentioned it so casually but it would be worth millions—four or five. Despite her father wanting his children to pay their way he'd bet she hadn't had to struggle as a student the way he had. No serving in a bar or doing late-night shelf-stacking shifts at the supermarket for her. She'd spent her spare time throwing wild parties. Getting arrested. Or maybe that was gossipy rumor, as she said. But she certainly hadn't been a quiet, unobtrusive member of the student body. If there was a buzz on campus she was usually involved.

Had she changed? The keys didn't inspire confidence.

Tess stood up and began stacking their plates and cutlery.

He said, "Thank you for that. I feel much better."

"Don't expect breakfast every morning. This was only because I thought you were a guest." She smiled. He laughed and picked up the empty fruit plate, balancing the milk jug and sugar bowl on top. He followed her into the house. She looked good in shorts. Gorgeous legs. She put the dirty plates on the bench and turned. "These can't go in the dishwasher."

"Noted. What time are you leaving for rehearsal?"

"About twelve thirty. Takes about thirty minutes depending on traffic."

"I'd like to go for a walk and get some fresh air into my lungs."

She glanced at the clock on the oven: 10:43. "I'll show you around first."

She took him on a grand tour starting with the formal dining room off the kitchen to the right. Then the laundry and back door that led, she said, to the garage and music studio. Back to the living area and up the passageway to the front door. First door on the right. "I practice in here. It was Daddy's study."

He saw a music stand with an open piece of music, the Mahler Symphony for the next concert. An upright piano. A dark wooden rolltop desk. Her viola in its case open on a small divan. Shelves laden with books and music, a sound system and a computer. A telephone. The walls were painted rich burgundy; the curtains dark patterned blue and black. A masculine room.

"Nice."

She moved on. "This is the living room. I don't use it." He'd glanced in earlier when Tess the whirlwind was chasing the dog and Ian brought him inside. He walked across to study the painting. Beautiful. "Original Charles Conder?"

"Yes." So casual. It would be worth a small fortune. And the sketches hanging alongside were by Australian artists he recognized.

Again she'd moved on while he gasped and did mental calculations. She stopped, pointing to a panel on the wall. "Here's the alarm. The door has to be shut before you can set it and you can only come in through this door or the alarm goes off. You've got twenty seconds to get out and the same to turn it off." Blue eyes looked up at him sternly from under the wispy bangs.

"I understand," he said solemnly. "What's the code?"

"It's 1812. Like the Tchaikovsky Overture. So's I can remember."

"Got it."

"Press this when the light goes green and when the beeps start, get out. Do you want to practice it?"

"No, I can manage. I've used alarms before. What about the dog? Doesn't he have to be outside?"

"Dogs," she corrected. "Yes. I forgot, they do."

"Dogs?"

"You haven't met Hannibal," she said in a very off-hand and disturbingly suspicious way.

Chapter Two

"No, I haven't." Two dogs?!

"He's around somewhere. He's old so he sleeps a lot. Can't move very fast, either."

Didn't sound too bad. Slow, decrepit, asleep most of the time. Infinitely better than that bouncing, yipping thing. He'd have to be wary when walking on the grass. Now they were powering through another door, which he'd assumed led into a bedroom but turned out to hide another hallway.

"Guest washroom. My bedroom." She indicated the second door on the right but didn't show him in. "Bathroom. Linen cupboards." On the left. "Two more bedrooms." Right and left at the end of the corridor.

"You could take in two more boarders. Pay off your car loan in no time."

"True, but I'd be in jail for life for murder so it'd be pointless."

"That bad, huh? I'd better be careful."

"You don't like living with people either."

"No but I don't resort to murder."

"We'll see, won't we?" she said with a sunny smile and a raised eyebrow.

"I think we'll be fine," he said doubtfully. "It's only a week."

"There's a rental crisis."

"Can't be too bad or you'd have a tenant." Or was there something else about her or the house he wasn't aware of? A ghost? Was she a secret drinker or did she indulge in satanic rituals? He trailed after her as she led him through the house again to the back door and outside. The laundry held that odd odor now. She didn't comment even though he sniffed ostentatiously.

"Like I said, I'm picky. Here's the garage." She waved an arm at the building with ivy crawling all over it and magnificent purple and red rhododendrons all along the side facing the garden. A high wall and security gate blocked access to the driveway and the street. He walked in through the open side door to see the cause of her enforced cohabitation. A silver Mercedes convertible sat smugly inside.

"Good heavens!"

"What?" She came to stand beside him, tense with alarm.

"You bought this?"

"Yes." Her body sagged as she exhaled in relief. "Gee, you frightened me! I thought something was wrong with it." She punched his arm playfully hard. "They're very good cars and I've always wanted a convertible."

"So have I, but it'll be years before I can afford one. If ever." He rubbed his upper arm. That ring was as good as a knuckle-duster.

"You can drive mine if you like," she said serenely.

"So my rent is paying for this?" Had she no sense of budgeting? But then, why should she? Daddy would have provided everything she desired.

"Yes. Partly. I call her the Diva because she's a very special lady."

He walked over to peer inside. The smell was pure luxury. Leather seats. Brand new. "I'm surprised you went for the four-seater rather than the roadster."

"No room for my viola or much luggage. I'm not a total idiot. I can be practical if necessary. Plus, she's cheaper."

She suddenly squatted down and peered under the car. The terrier licked her face and she shoved him away.

"What are you looking for? It's not dripping oil already, is it?"

She jumped to her feet in one easy movement. "I was checking for Hannibal so we don't shut him in. He likes to lie under things. Come on." She grabbed his arm and pulled him along the path to another door at the rear of the garage. "Daddy had this built when I was at school. So I could practice and not disturb anyone."

David stifled a gasp of surprise at the beautifully equipped studio she revealed. A baby grand piano occupied one corner. Several solid black music stands clustered in another. Recording and sound equipment sat on a long bench. Floor-to-ceiling shelving housed vinyl records, CDs, books, videos, and music. He counted half a dozen chairs and enough open floor space to rehearse an ensemble or give a small recital.

"And you don't use it?" he asked in amazement. He'd practiced in his bedroom with one brother yelling to their mother, "Tell him to shut up," another one playing electric guitar in the garage, and often as not the TV blaring or Dad and his eldest brother revving an engine in the backyard.

"No, I'd rather be inside. It's a bit isolated out here. You can use it though." Another brilliant smile.

"I most definitely will. Thank you." He returned the smile and she held his gaze a moment. Almost frozen in place. She opened her mouth and the tip of her tongue emerged to moisten her lower lip, then her teeth rubbed gently and pulled the soft red lip inside. She looked away and stepped around him quickly.

"I should do some practice before rehearsal. We're doing Mahler Five." Her voice sounded odd, strained. "Not a good look for the Principal to get the dots wrong."

"You go ahead. I'll go for that walk and be back before you leave."

"Take Fid with you," she threw over her shoulder. "I'll get his lead."

The dog yipped with excitement and ran around in circles. Great. Just what he wanted.

Tess clicked the remote and the roller door rumbled into place, securing her beautiful Mercedes for the night. The Diva. Aaron thought she was insane naming her cars. Lots of people did; it wasn't mad at all. David would probably laugh at her too. He was still basically very serious and appeared to think she was a flake because he gave her some very strange looks. But he seemed to like her house. As did everyone. Not enough to share with her, though.

Except Aaron, but she didn't want to share with him because he would see it as a step toward a more permanent relationship, and she didn't. Even though, technically, sharing was living together. But not the way he wanted, or said he wanted. Really what he desired wasn't her so much as to live in the house, so he could boast about the address and living in Lionel Fuller's home. He didn't love her any more than she loved him, but if she let him establish himself there'd be no shifting him. She didn't want a housemate on those terms.

After Raoul, she wasn't rushing into anything involving a man who said he loved her.

What would Aaron say when he discovered David in residence? He'd be pretty miffed, that's for sure. If she let him believe David was her new love, he may finally get the message. It wouldn't be fibbing. Not really. It'd just be not explaining. Except they'd have to have had a whirlwind love-at-first-sight affair because there was no hiding the fact that David had just arrived in Sydney. And Aaron knew all about Raoul and how bruised she was. Not a good plan. Scrap that.

Anyway, Aaron knew she wanted a tenant and David was only staying a week. So far.

She took her viola and the bag of groceries from the rear seat. Ian had asked how David had settled in and she told him truthfully, "Very well." Then she added, "He thought he was my guest for a few days. Why didn't you tell him I wanted a rent-paying tenant?"

He said, evasively to her way of thinking, "I thought you could sort that out between you. He may not have wanted to stay more than a night for all I knew. Is he?"

"He's staying a week, then we'll see."

"Really?" His hastily hidden surprise stung.

"Yes. Why not?" she demanded.

Then he was his usual bland, efficient politeness. "No reason. He didn't want to share, that's all. He made it very clear. He wanted a two-bedroom place in the inner city."

"He won't find anything as good as my place for the rent. You'll need to pay me for this week." She sent him a defiant look down her nose. Daddy said she had the Fuller nose—straight and clearly defined. Aristocratic.

"Fine. It'll be in your pay."

Something about the way he shifted his gaze when she tried to look him in the eye was unsettling. Stuff him. As he said, she and David sorted it out so it wasn't his business anymore apart from coughing up the money.

As she locked the garage door, Fid came bounding from the bushes along the back fence uttering yips of delight. "Hello, baby," she cried. "How are you?" He bounced up and down licking and wiggling, then shot off across the lawn. "Where's Hannibal?" He didn't answer but raced back and circled her feet.

A slight unease at the thought of Hannibal made her bite her lower lip gently. Had David met him yet? He wasn't a dog person. Hannibal strained even a dog lover's goodwill. He wasn't at all keen on Fid but did deign to take him out walking and they came back united and in good spirits. Fid was very obedient on the lead and loved his walks. Nothing could really go wrong there. But Hannibal . . .

She pushed opened the back door and called, "I'm home."

No reply. The house was quiet. No sign of David in the family room or on the terrace. He'd washed up the breakfast dishes and put them away. Fulfilling his part of the deal already even though she'd really meant to clear up before she left, but hadn't. He'd folded the newspaper she'd left spread all over the dining table too, and today's mail sat neatly next to it. She unloaded the contents of her shopping bag into the fridge, took her viola to the study, and went to wash her hands and use the bathroom.

"Where is he, Fid?"

Fid grinned adoringly and panted.

A quick peep into the living room confirmed he wasn't there either. Hannibal was, though. He stood gazing solemnly out the front window surrounded by a haze of noxious fumes and barely moved when she walked over to stroke his graying black head and ruffle his ears. "Hello, old man."

One bleary eye blinked and he turned his head slightly to assess the intruder. A distant rumble indicated he was on duty, growling to protect the property. "Good boy," she said and left him to it. He hardly had any teeth left. Maybe the mush he ate caused the toxic intestinal gases.

In the kitchen Tess pulled out a packet of cracker biscuits and a tub of cream cheese sweet chili dip. Munching, she contemplated her situation. If she could convince David that this was the best place to live for at least— what? She stuck a cracker into the dip and scooped up a big mouthful. About ten years? That's what it would take to clear her debt. He'd never stay that long.

She maneuvered her tongue around the inside of her teeth removing cracker debris. Take it one week at a time. He was house hunting; living here would spoil him for the dodgy, cramped places he'd be inspecting. Wait it out. Be cool.

She was about as good at being cool as she was at handling money and being tidy. Stu would have fifty fits when he found out about the Diva and then he'd know about the boarder situation. She froze. Someone may have already told him. Aaron? No. He knew she'd been considering buying the Diva but didn't know she'd sealed the deal because she deliberately hadn't discussed finances with him. Someone from the orchestra? No. Even though she'd been seeking out the best rates with ongoing advice from Tim in percussion, none of them knew Stu. The whole thing could be a fait accompli before he found out. She need only contribute a small part of her wages and the Diva would be paid for in no time.

Except she hadn't figured on having trouble finding a boarder. But she had one now and she aimed to keep him! Bonus that he was the gorgeous David Montgomery. And even if by some freak chance Stu did find out, he couldn't possibly invoke that stupid, stupid will clause. That was plain spite on Daddy's part. Stu wouldn't evict her, not his sister.

She pushed herself away from the bench where she'd been lounging and eating. Where was David? Had he stumbled across Hannibal and decamped? No. He wouldn't go off and leave the house unlocked.

Asleep? Disastrous! He mustn't sleep too long or he'd be awake all night and never adjust. She grabbed another cracker with a dollop of dip and headed for his room. "Stay!" she said to Fid, who'd eagerly rushed to accompany her. Didn't want to upset David. Must keep Fid away as much as possible. It had all been going very well so far. Don't know why Ian was so surprised.

She tapped on the closed bedroom door then, receiving no answer, opened it and peeped in. Just as she'd thought. Dead to the world. Cripes he was good-looking! Tess stepped closer to the bed almost holding her breath at the magnificence of him. Here in her house. In her bed. One of her beds. Sharing with her. Who'd have thought it all those years ago. Aloof David Montgomery lying bare-chested in her bed. Bare-chested? He was! He'd pushed the quilt back and lay under the lavender gray sheet. Which came to stomach level.

What a stomach! Tanned, flat, rising and falling gently with each slumberous breath. Tess wrenched her eyes away from the outline of his lower body. She swallowed and placed her palms flat against her throbbing cheeks, forgetting one hand held a cracker with dip. Crumbs dropped to the floor, cool creamy dip blobbed on her chin.

"Whoops." She dropped to the floor and scrabbled for the broken pieces of cracker at the same time wiping dip from her chin and licking it from her finger.

The bed creaked, bedclothes rustled. A body stirred. Lay still. She stood up slowly and released the handful of crumbs into the pocket of her slacks. He was still asleep. On his side now, broad back turned her way. A quick peek in the dressing table mirror confirmed she'd cleaned up successfully. How to go about this? He had to be woken.

She strode to the door and knocked loudly. Nothing. "David," she called. "Wake up." Nothing.

She marched to the bed. He was right in the middle so she put one knee on the edge and leaned across to grasp his shoulder. Bare skin. Warm. Muscular. Her breath caught. Exhaled in a rush. "David." A croaky sound. She cleared her throat. "David." A firm shake. He rolled over to face her, lying on his back, eyes flickering open then shut again. "David, you can't sleep now."

"Hdgrmmnph," he said.

Now they were getting somewhere. "Wake up."

The eyes opened and fixed on her face. He clearly had no idea who she was or where he was.

"I'm Tess," she said helpfully. "You're in my house. In Sydney."

"Tess," he murmured. A slow smile spread across his face. "Am I in your bed?" The eyelids drooped.

She nodded because her voice had shut down in her throat. He reached out a gentle hand and touched her face. "You're very beautiful." His eyes closed completely and his breathing deepened.

"David!"

His eyes flicked open. This time he was awake properly. Frowning in annoyance. "Tess?"

"You can't sleep any more."

"What?" He rubbed a hand across his face and yawned. "I dreamed . . . what time is it?"

"Nearly six. How long have you been asleep?"

"Couple of hours." He stared at her. She was sitting

on his bed, she realized. Close. So close he could reach out and touch her cheek. He thought he'd been dreaming. Who did he think was beautiful? "Why did you wake me?" His growl was akin to Hannibal's.

She slid off the bed. "If you sleep any longer you won't sleep tonight."

"I can make these decisions for myself, thank you." He didn't look at all grateful for her concern; he looked downright angry. "I set the alarm for six thirty."

"Sorry," she said stiffly. "Just trying to be helpful." Her eyes would keep straying to his chest. He should pull the sheet up. But he didn't, he just kept staring, or rather glaring, at her. Waiting for her to leave.

"Thank you."

She backed toward the door, bumped into it, turned and fled.

"Shut the door," he bellowed. "Please." Definitely an afterthought.

Twenty minutes later he entered the kitchen wearing the shirt and slacks from earlier. Tess looked up warily from the tabouli salad she was spooning from the plastic supermarket container into a serving bowl. He hadn't bothered shaving the fuzz of dark stubble, and with tiredness sinking his dark eyes and shadowing his face, he looked indescribably sexy.

"I bought salad and cold chicken on the way home." She had to forcibly remove the image of his bare chest from her mind. "We can eat whenever you like."

"Fine." He went to the fridge and removed a jug of

water. He must have put that in there because she certainly hadn't. He poured himself a glass. "Want one?"

She shook her head. "I have your key. It's there." She indicated with the spoon. Bits of parsley fell to the granite surface. He walked around the bench and picked up the shiny little key and slipped it into his pocket.

"I had three done. Plenty of spares," she said but he didn't smile.

He drank some chilled water. "Thanks." Then he picked up the sponge and began wiping spilled tabouli and cracker crumbs into a finicky little pile.

"The orchestra is having a get-to-know-you barbecue lunch on Sunday. That's getting to know *you*. We already know each other. At Stanislav Mazur's place in Lane Cove. He's first desk next to you."

"That's nice," he said tersely. "Are you going?" He dumped the debris into the bin.

Her head shot up in surprise. "Of course. Why wouldn't I?"

He shrugged. "Can I have a lift? Please?" He rinsed his hands under the tap and looked around.

She grinned. Did he think she'd drive off and leave him to catch a cab? "You can drive if you like." She opened a drawer, pulled out a handtowel, and tossed it to him.

"Thanks. I'll need to get my U.S. license switched."

"Do you need to? Isn't your license valid here?"

"I'm not sure, but I don't want to drive illegally." He hung the towel neatly on the oven door.

She took potato salad from the fridge. "Who'd know? If you get pulled over, plead ignorance."

David shook his head in disbelief. "That might work for you but not me."

She bit back on the irritation. He sounded so pompous. What did he think she was? A teenage hooligan? "Go and check it out on the Web, then. Use the computer in the study."

"I will. I'd like to check my e-mail too, if that's all right?"

"Of course. You live here."

"But it's your computer."

"I have a laptop as well. We can share the computer," she said. For heaven's sake! She may not be keen on sharing the house but she wasn't going to be picky about who can use what now that he was here.

He started toward the study but stopped. "Your brother called, by the way."

Stuart. Cripes! "What did he want?"

"He'll call again tonight." He studied her expression with a puzzled frown. "What's the matter?"

"What did he say when you answered?" Her fingers had gone all stiff and clumsy as she scraped potato salad into a dish. Blobs fell on to the bench top.

" 'Is Tess there?' " He stared pointedly at the mess she'd made on his clean bench.

She snorted. "No, did he ask who you were?" The spoon fell with a clatter. Tess reached for the sponge and smeared mayonnaise in streaky swipes across the shiny granite.

"Yes and I told him." He was watching her curiously, making her even more awkward.

"What did you tell him?" Her stomach turned to lead, her lungs almost ceased working. If Stuart discovered she was taking in boarders he'd have a conniption fit, and if he found out why she'd be in so much trouble . . .

"I said, 'I'm David Montgomery and I'm staying here for a few days until I find my own place.' "

She released the pent-up breath she hadn't realized she was holding, and sagged against the bench.

"Tess? What are you up to?" He stepped closer, stern faced. A familiar defiance rose from within. Always that suspicion—her father, her brother, her teachers, Aaron, her father's lawyers, and now David—they all thought she was hiding some mischief, sneakily doing something she shouldn't, that she was a naughty little girl up to no good. Nobody trusted her to do the right thing without supervision.

She straightened her spine and her voice emerged cool and distant. "Nothing. I'm not up to anything."

David tilted his head doubtfully. She gritted her teeth, ready for the next assault. But his eyes were kind if distant. He wasn't involved at all in her life. He wouldn't care what she did. He was just rooming here. She dropped her gaze to the mess on the bench. "Stu thinks I'm a total nitwit where money's concerned and compared to him and Daddy, I am. He wouldn't like the idea of people renting rooms here, that's all." She jerked her eyes back to his face. "But it's ridiculous. I'm a responsible adult. He still thinks I'm a child—his baby sister."

"So," David said, connecting dots way faster then a jet-lagged man should be capable of. "You're scared he'll find out you've bought that expensive car and need to take in boarders to help pay it off." He fixed his eyes on hers. She couldn't look away.

Tess twisted her face in an effort to reword that to sound less . . . less . . . accurate and more adult, but couldn't. "Yes."

He stretched out a hand and patted her shoulder the way her father used to do. "Don't worry. My lips are sealed. I'm a guest." He turned as he went through the study door and said, "He sounded rather impressed when I told him I was the new concert master so you may earn a few Brownie points there."

Tess glared at his retreating back. Men! All the same. They all thought they knew best about everything. David thought she was a child too and he'd sounded exactly like her father for a freaky moment when he asked what she was up to. And that thing about the driver's license. She'd bet there'd be some time allowance to have a valid license changed over. He wouldn't be driving illegally and she wouldn't expect him to, or do it herself.

But at least he'd cheered up. He apparently didn't hold grudges.

His head almost instantly reappeared around the study door with a hideously contorted expression. "There's the most horrendous pong in here. What is it? Drains?"

"No." She sucked in air through tight lips. Time to come clean. "It's Hannibal. He has a . . . a . . . gas problem. I told you he was old," she added defensively as David's face twisted into even more gargoyle-like horror. He marched across to the open terrace doors and took a few deep cleansing breaths.

"Gas problem?" he asked when he returned. "Are you sure he hasn't died? Underneath something?"

"Of course he hasn't died. He was in the living room when I came home. Is he in the study?"

"He's been in there," he said through gritted teeth. "I'll do my e-mails later when the miasma has cleared."

"Would you like a cold drink or a beer?" Tess asked brightly. That hadn't gone nearly as badly as it might have. He hadn't rushed to pack his bag.

"A beer, thanks. No wonder you can't find a housemate." David perched himself on one of the high stools and leaned one arm on the bench opposite her. Tess placed the remains of the chili dip and crackers in front of him. She removed a beer from the fridge and handed it to him silently. He twisted the cap off, tipped the bottle toward her in acknowledgment, and drank.

Tess poured herself more iced water. Was he right? Had Hannibal put off that nice friend of Grace's? She'd seemed an ideal companion but had regretfully declined, giving a very vague reason. And Hannibal *had* materialized right outside her bedroom when she was looking it over. She'd ask Grace on Sunday at the barbecue.

The phone rang. Tess answered without thinking, belatedly thought and almost panicked in case it was Stuart and she hadn't prepared herself. But it wasn't. She passed the receiver to David. "It's Ian."

He smiled as if he knew what she'd been imagining and took the phone and his beer out to the terrace.

Fifteen minutes later he came back inside after wandering about the garden nattering nonstop. Tess sat curled up on the lounge watching the news on TV. He glanced at the screen as he dropped into a chair.

"Any fresh disasters I should know about? I haven't seen the news for days."

"The usual. Like to eat soon?"

"Yes, please."

Tess stood up and went to the kitchen. Everything was ready on the bench. "I thought we could eat outside again. I love eating out there when the weather is good. Which it is most of the time. Except when it rains, of course. We've had a few terrific thunderstorms. Springtime."

"Fine." He helped ferry food and plates out to the terrace. Fid watched the preparations eagerly.

When they were eating, with Fid lurking under the table, David said, "Ian rang to check I'd settled in with you all right."

"I told him you had. What did you say?"

He swallowed a mouthful. "I said very well. So far."

"So far? What do you mean so far?" Her fork stopped midway to the plate of chicken.

"I've only been here a matter of hours. Anything could happen."

"Nothing will." Tess speared a piece of cold chicken and then another. What was this? A universal conspiracy against living with her?

"No more Hannibal-type surprises tucked away?"

"No!" Tess glanced up and met his gaze full-on. His eyes were sparkling with amusement. He was laughing at her. Fid nudged her ankle hopefully. "Go away," she said to him.

"Can I finish dinner first?"

Tess cried, shocked, "Not you! I was talking to Fid."

He laughed outright. "I know, I was teasing you."

Tess laughed too but her laughter was in surprise that he was laughing. And that he'd teased her. Almost like flirting. The David she remembered was far too serious to flirt. But that was years ago. She'd changed, even if her brother didn't think so, and so, presumably, had David. He was relaxing. Good sign. Very good sign.

And my goodness, wasn't he attractive when he laughed?

"Like to walk down to the beach after dinner?" she asked, still smiling. She couldn't stop herself from grinning at him. He'd think she was demented. "It's not far, only about ten minutes."

"I would but I'd like to take advantage of your music studio and do some practice."

Practice! Of course. He wouldn't have touched his violin for at least two days. "Yes, you're playing the Beethoven Concerto with us! I'm so looking forward to that."

"Are you?" He suddenly looked boyishly pleased in the face of her enthusiasm.

"Of course. The whole orchestra is looking forward to hearing you perform. You were the best player by far when we were students and I've got two of your recordings. You can autograph them for me." Was he kidding? He was a seriously world-class violinist and the directors of the City had been delighted when he applied for the position as concert master. It had been a done deal as soon as they knew he wanted the job. They wouldn't pay a week's rent for anyone else joining the band.

"I'd better get some work done, in that case. Don't want to disappoint anyone."

He wouldn't disappoint. David Montgomery knew exactly how good he was but the laughter had gone and the remark uttered in complete seriousness and with a worried frown reminded Tess that this man was still as focused and driven as he ever was.

Chapter Three

Tess went for her walk with Fid trotting happily beside her, and came home in plenty of time to watch *The Philadelphia Story* on TV. David was practicing. The music studio had been made soundproof and any playing was inaudible in the house but Tess fed the dogs and sat on the back step for fifteen minutes, listening. The sound was muted but the talent wasn't in any way diminished by jet lag or unfamiliar surroundings. He sounded marvelous.

Eventually she roused herself. The movie was due to start. She checked Hannibal's kennel tucked around the rear of the studio near the washing line. He was curled up snoring. "Time for bed," she told Fid. He sat obediently in front of his own kennel. "Good boy."

The back door opened and closed when Cary Grant

was finally reclaiming Katharine Hepburn on the very brink of her marriage to the upper-class loser.

Tess tore her attention but not her eyes reluctantly from the scene when David said, "Do the dogs stay outside at night?"

"Yes."

"That's a surprise. I thought they'd sleep in your bed."

"No." Now Cary was telling Katharine to marry him again instead. What a fabulous movie.

"Or at the very least have a place in the laundry."

She glanced at him and said abruptly, "My father hated dogs in the house. He said their job was to guard the property. Now shush."

"What's the movie?"

"*The Philadelphia Story.* Shh."

He sat down. "It's in black-and-white."

"Mmm. Shhhh."

He picked up the folded TV guide and rustled the pages as he flipped through. "Not much on." He tossed it aside.

The credits rolled. Tess flicked the Off button. She turned to the intruder. "I love that movie, it's a classic, and you spoiled the ending."

"But you've seen it before so you know the ending."

"That's not the point."

"Are you going to murder me?" He grinned at her. He was uncommonly cheerful.

She wasn't going to acknowledge that crack. Murder

wasn't what sprang to mind when he smiled at her like that. "Practice go well?"

The grin widened and he leaned forward enthusiastically. "Excellent. The acoustics in that room are perfect. It's an amazing room."

"I know. It was specifically engineered and sound-proofed."

He shook his head in disbelief. "And you prefer to practice in the study?" He eyed her speculatively and folded his arms behind his head, then stretched them up with fingers interlocked.

Tess stood up. "Yep. I'm going to bed. I have a tai chi class in the morning so I'll be out early. Back around nine."

"Tai chi?" His arms dropped to his lap. He couldn't hide the surprise.

"Yes, why not? It's good for musicians. I have a problem with my shoulder sometimes." She glared at him, daring him to say what she suspected he'd been thinking. Tess do something as esoteric and philosophical as tai chi? The Party Girl? He made a good recovery.

"I've thought of taking that up. You'll have to show me some."

Her defiance drained away and suddenly she was self-conscious under his scrutiny. "I don't know enough yet and I'm not very good at it."

His brown eyes softened and his lips curved slightly.

"Bringing breakfast home with you?" Her knees wobbled under the onslaught of charm. How would she stand a week of this proximity without behaving wantonly and embarrassing them both? It'd confirm his erroneous idea of her as a freewheeling party girl, that's for sure if she attempted to seduce him.

"I could call in at the bakery."

"Please do. I normally have cereal and fruit but those croissants are very good. As a treat."

"Good night." She turned to go.

He said in a much different tone, serious, no hint of teasing, "Thanks for taking me in at such short notice, Tess. I appreciate it."

"No worries. Don't stay up too late or you'll be messed up tomorrow."

"No, I'm pretty tired. Good night."

It was all she could do not to throw herself into his lap and press her mouth onto those smiling lips. Instead she walked unsteadily along the hallway and closed herself in her bedroom where she sat on her bed, breathing hard. Maybe having him in the house was not such a good plan after all. It may turn out to be some exquisite kind of torture. Self-denial wasn't her strong suit.

"I've been taking stock of your supplies." David poured himself more tea and lounged back in his chair. While she was out he'd sliced the remaining melon and pineapple, prepared the tea, and set the outdoor table for breakfast. Better than a maid. If he was as organized and house-trained as this, sharing might be very good value. "We need to go food shopping. I've made a list."

"Yes, specially if you're preparing dinner tonight," she said lazily. Another sunny spring morning to start what she had thought would be a dullish weekend. No concerts, no rehearsals, and with Lauren overseas the social outings and girls' gossip sessions on the phone had stalled. Now, with a barbecue to look forward to tomorrow and a pleasant day hanging out with David today, things were looking up. Grocery shopping may even be enjoyable rather than the chore it always was.

He put his cup down. "Oh sorry. Didn't I mention? Ian invited me to have dinner with him and Viktor Zakharoff and the directors."

"No." Was that disappointment that she had to share him with the world? But she'd rather eat alone than sit through a dinner with that lot. Apart from Viktor, who was fascinating and impossibly handsome in a dark Russian way, but unshakably devoted to his wife. "That'll be fun."

He raised an eyebrow. "Meaning?"

"Nothing. I don't have much to do with any of them. As little as possible, actually." David wasn't impressed, she could tell by his expression if not by his next comment.

"You're Principal Viola, a section leader. It's your job to be interested in the running of the orchestra," he said with a disapproving narrowing of the eyes. Add dereliction of duty to the Party Girl's misdemeanor list.

"I am interested but I think you're overestimating the importance of Principal Viola in the grand scheme of things." She broke off a piece of croissant and flipped it in the air toward Fid, who snapped it up before it hit the ground.

"I don't think that's very good for him." David frowned. "Dogs shouldn't eat pastry."

"Hasn't harmed him yet." She sent another piece Fid's way. What did he know about dogs? He didn't even like them.

David studiously sipped tea with a blank expression. Whoops! Better not antagonize him, a boarder in the house was worth two not in the house.

"Viktor is a terrific conductor." He couldn't argue with that.

"Yes, he was one of the reasons I applied for this position."

"He works us very hard."

"Good. I like that."

"So do I and he has very strict rules in rehearsal. No chatting, for example."

David glanced at her with the hint of a smile. "You must find that difficult."

"I do not!" Curses. He was laughing at her again. Teasing. Tess clammed her mouth shut. He piled apricot jam onto his last piece of croissant but a chuckle escaped before he shoved it into his mouth. Fid jumped up from under the table and ran around to his side, grinning, wanting to join in the fun. David actually patted

Fid's head. The phone rang inside and she leaped up to answer it, leaving the pair of them to it.

"Hello, babe." Aaron. No contact from him for at least a week.

"Hello. How are you?" Maybe they could do something tonight.

"Fine. How about spending the day on Jean-Pierre's yacht? You don't have a rehearsal or anything, do you? I can be there in fifteen minutes."

Fifteen minutes? Where was he? She glanced at David lolling in his chair with his eyes closed enjoying the peaceful morning. "No, but I'm about to go grocery shopping."

"Oh, forget that!"

Tess laughed. Jean-Pierre's yacht was more of a luxury cruiser. He referred to it as the Champagne Float.

David tried not to eavesdrop but she made no attempt to lower her voice or keep the conversation private. The way she said "grocery shopping" implied it was the lowest activity she could imagine. Tess would have friends. Lots of them. She was probably doing something tonight. Something she considered far more entertaining than dinner with the orchestra's directors. But he was looking forward to it.

He'd taken a prestigious position and meant to fulfill his duties with pride and attention to detail. One of his childhood ambitions had been to lead the City Symphony. Ever since the orchestra had done a country tour and his parents drove all the way to Wagga Wagga to give their young sons a night of culture. His brothers had fidgeted but he'd been spellbound and not least by the man who played the lead violin. Oscar Stevenson had also been soloist in the Beethoven Violin Concerto.

On the way home in the car he'd announced, "I'm going to do that one day," to the derision of his brothers and the quietly amused encouragement of his parents. Now that ambition had been realized and he certainly wasn't taking the achievement as lightly as Tess seemed to take hers. But then he'd had to practice like a demon to get where he was. Hours of arm-aching, finger-numbing work. He'd started a few years later than most, enduring the jokes and scathing comments from his classmates and friends, all more interested in football and country music than orchestras and violin lessons.

Tess' voice faded on laughter as she moved farther into the kitchen. What a case she was. This week would be entertaining and that music studio more than made up for any oddities and shortcomings of the landlady and pets. It provided the perfect venue for undisturbed, concentrated practice before making his debut with the orchestra, his introduction to Sydney's critical musical world, proving himself worthy of the position. He'd assumed he'd have to find a room at the orchestra's rehearsal hall because most rental places didn't welcome hours of violin playing. No, this had been a stroke of great good fortune. But he couldn't live with her noisy untidiness for any longer than a week.

A rough wet tongue scraped the back of his hand. He

tousled Fid's soft ears. The dog wasn't too bad. Good company on a walk and very obedient. Better have a look at the For Rent ads. He stood up and began stacking the tray with their breakfast dishes. The newspaper was scattered all over the dining table where Tess had left it after a cursory rummage through it after her return from tai chi. That messiness was definitely not endearing. Yesterday's opened mail lay strewn about—empty envelopes, a credit card statement, something from the local council, a real estate agent flyer. She was here, she could clean it up.

She was leaning against the bench with the phone against one ear saying mournfully, "Sorry, I really can't, Aaron. I have a guest." She giggled. Aaron must have replied because she said, "No, but I hope so. Bye-bye." Even the baggy Indian cotton pants and loose shirt she'd worn to tai chi couldn't hide the fact she had a sensational body.

"Don't change any plans because of me," David said stiffly. What was she hoping? He wouldn't stay or he would? He put the tray down and started unloading. Tess lolled with her arms folded, watching.

"I'm not. Aaron thinks he can ring up and invite me out any old time and I'll drop everything and go." She tilted her head, considering, then smiled. "Come to think of it, I usually do. Unless we have rehearsals or a concert."

"Is he your boyfriend?"

"No. He wants to move in here though."

"As a boarder?" He filled the sink with water for the cups and saucers. Was she going to wield the tea towel? "Put rubber gloves on the list."

Tess picked up the pencil he'd left on the bench. He'd had to hunt high and low for pencil and paper, eventually finding them in the study. She scrawled something down. "He wouldn't see it that way but I don't want to live with him in any sense. I like my independence and I told you I was picky."

"But I pass muster?" He picked up the sponge. Detergent was harsh on his skin; he'd have to be careful just before a performance. Didn't want any eczema or dryness to interfere with his preparation.

Tess smiled. "So far." The smile disappeared. "But you're different. I mean your reasons for being here are different. Aaron wants to live here because of the house, not me. I doubt whether he'd want to live with me if I lived in a tiny unit in Redfern. Or if I suggested I move in with him. He's never suggested that. He has an apartment in Chatswood."

"You can't blame him. It *is* a fantastic house." He grinned to take the edge off the remark and the fact that he was guilty of exactly the same motivation, albeit inadvertently. And for at most, a week.

Tess ran her fingertip along the smooth granite, tracing an invisible pattern. When she met his eyes her expression was somber and for the first time in their brief acquaintance she looked vulnerable. "I've learned over the years to suss out who likes me for me and who likes me for what I own or who my father was."

"Who was he exactly?" David carefully rinsed the cups and placed them on the drainer. "Dry these."

"Won't they dry by themselves? I don't know why you did them anyway. I usually leave them until there's enough to make it worthwhile running the dishwasher." Which would be when she ran out of crockery. Tess shoved away from the bench and wandered across to the table. She sat down and turned a page or two of the paper. "My father was Lionel Fuller."

"Don't know the name, I'm afraid."

Tess looked at him curiously. "Really?"

"Really." David snatched the tea towel from the rack and began drying a saucer. "Should I?"

She shrugged. "Daddy was a banker. He had a lot of influence—stock market, parliament, business. You name it. I'm surprised you haven't heard of him even just from the news. Especially when he died."

"I've never been very interested in big business, high finance," he said. "And I've been overseas for the last eight years. Australia barely rates a mention anywhere else unless it's to do with some actor or TV star. Or a natural disaster."

He swiped the towel across another saucer. Lazy so-and-so . . . She was going to do her share, daughter of the famous Lionel Fuller or not!

The last cup went back into place in the cupboard.

David hung the damp tea towel on the oven door and joined Tess at the table. She sat with one hand supporting her chin, studying the crossword.

"What's a mantle of animal skins starting with *k*?"

"No idea. I need to look at the For Rents."

"You can stay here as long as you like." But she gave up on the crossword and found the relevant section of the paper.

"A week will be plenty long enough."

"Am I that awful?"

He glanced up quickly. She was smiling that lovely smile. Expecting him to deny it. He flipped through the muddle of pages, frowning, looking for the rental ads. Keeping any unwanted sparks of desire at bay. "You're untidy, you don't help wash up, and you talk too much. Plus your dog stinks."

"But *apart* from that."

He shook his head and didn't reply. He found the listings. "Plenty to choose from."

"They'll all be rubbish," Tess replied. "Are we going shopping? I need to practice the Mahler."

"So do I, but Beethoven. I'll call some agents now and if we go after that I can practice for an hour or two and maybe do some apartment hunting this afternoon. You'll have the afternoon to yourself."

"How will you get around?"

"Taxi."

Tess sighed ostentatiously. "Would you like me to come?"

"You don't have to. I'm sure you have other, far more interesting things to do." Did he want her along? The offer of transport was kind but would she be a help or a hindrance? She was certainly distracting. He wanted to touch his fingers to that soft cheek.

"I don't. I'll enjoy proving myself right. For the money I'm charging, you won't find anywhere near as good." She began quoting the desirable features. "Private room and bathroom in a fully furnished luxury house with large garden. Harborside suburb with water views. Fully equipped music studio for your own private use. Lockup garage space if you own a car. One very pleasant, friendly, musical cotenant who is also land-lady."

David laughed. "You forgot to add 'bring your own gas mask.' "

"Hannibal's not that bad."

"Yes he is. You know—I haven't seen him yet. I just have your word that he exists."

"Of course he exists! Where do you think the smell comes from?"

"I try not to think about it at all."

She giggled, a throaty sexy sound. "He's like the Phantom."

"Ghost Who Walks."

"Yes, you never know where he's going to appear next."

"Believe me, he's not like the Phantom. I was a big Phantom fan."

"I wasn't, Stu was. I preferred Daffy Duck." Tess stood up. "Call me when you're ready to leave. I'll go and make sure Fid and the Phantom are outside." He couldn't drag his eyes from her as she sashayed from the room. The sooner he found his own place, the better. An attraction to Tess with all the ensuing complications would be the utmost folly.

Tess drove as David had expected. Confidently but fast to the point of white knuckles and hair standing straight up in shock. She also switched on the stereo system and they barreled through leafy respectable Mosman with the top down leaving a trail of violent rock music pulsating in the warm air behind them.

"Isn't tai chi supposed to make you slow down?" he yelled, hanging on grimly as they zoomed around a sharp corner almost on two wheels.

"I told you I'm not very good at it," she shouted. "Do you want to drive?"

"I'd love to but not today, thanks."

"Well don't tell me how to." She threw him a grin.

David wisely decided not to respond to that. Her car was a treat to ride in, despite the mad driver and the sound accompaniment. He'd love the chance to get behind the wheel. They roared into the shopping center parking area and came to rest like a butterfly between two large four-wheel-drive family mobiles.

The deafening music ceased abruptly. "Isn't the Diva fabulous!" she cried.

"I think so. I'm still waiting for my stomach to catch up."

"We should take her out for a spin on the freeway. Let her rip." She opened the door and jumped out.

"Maybe *you* could." David got out more sedately and joined her. She pulled a bundle of green bags from behind the seat and headed to the supermarket.

"Come on, David, don't be such a stodge. You'd love to have a go, wouldn't you? See how she handles on the open road? She's very restricted in the city. She wants to fly." Tess' arms flew wide almost connecting with a grocery laden passerby.

"How long have you had it?"

"Two weeks. I couldn't go anywhere last weekend. We had two concerts and this weekend is a write-off too."

"Surely one of your friends would go out with you. Aaron?" Anyone whose hearing wasn't fully functional.

"Yes. But I thought you might like to."

"I don't want to put myself in any danger until after I've played the Beethoven." Physically, mentally, or aurally.

"Danger?" Indignant, she stopped abruptly but laughed when she realized he was joking. But only half-joking. His nerves wouldn't stand an outing with Tess behind the wheel testing the Diva's potential for speed, which would be considerable. "Chicken." Smiling derision. "Got the list?"

The drive home was marginally more controlled owing to the bags of shopping stacked on the rear seat.

David adjusted the volume control and brought whoever it was down to a roar before they got properly started.

"Don't you like the Stones?"

"The Rolling Stones?"

"Yes, that's their new album. I went to see them when they toured last year. Wow! What a fabulous night. Incredible. They're all in their sixties and they have so much energy." She was virtually bouncing in her seat with the memory of it all.

"My parents were Beatles fans," he said in an effort to appear semi-knowledgeable. He'd be hard-pressed to name a Rolling Stones song.

"I have some Beatles CDs but I prefer the Stones. They're much dirtier."

"I'm not a pop music fan."

"This is rock not pop."

"Oh." There was a difference?

"Do you only listen to classical music?"

"Yes, mainly."

"I'll have to educate you," she said cheerfully.

"Will you?"

"If we're going to share we need to like the same music."

"We're not going to share, Tess, remember? I'm only staying a week and we do like the same music. Classical." And what a long week it was going to be if she insisted on broadening his musical tastes. Those agents he'd spoken to better have some good properties lined up for viewing this afternoon.

"Like to go for a swim?" Tess asked as they lugged groceries into the house. "Before we practice?"

"Sounds good but I'm suddenly feeling very tired." The change in time zones was catching him at odd moments. He'd woken at four that morning but stayed in bed hoping to sleep again. He hadn't.

"It'll wake you up."

"Maybe it will. All right, but only half an hour or so."

She dumped her bags on the kitchen floor. "Let's go! It's a ten-minute walk down to Balmoral Beach."

"What about this?" He gestured at the pile of groceries.

She paused. "Better put the cold stuff in the fridge, there's not much. The rest can wait till we get back." She was already halfway to her room.

David hoisted the bag of cold things onto the bench. "Feel like helping?" he muttered and began stacking yogurt in the fridge.

Tess reappeared in shorts and a cutoff tank top with a red tote bag and beach towel slung over her shoulder, as he finished putting the vegetables in the crisper.

"Aren't you ready yet?" she cried. "Come on. Leave that."

"You can finish putting this away while I change." He folded an empty green bag flat.

Tess stared at him for a moment but he glared right back at her with the compressed shopping bag clutched in one firm hand. He was serious. Blimey! She bent down and grabbed a tin of dog food. Talk about anal-retentive!

He was like a prison guard. He went away after watching for a moment in case she slacked off.

He came back in white shorts and a navy blue T-shirt holding a blue-and-yellow striped towel in one hand.

"Do you have sunscreen I can use?"

Tess dragged her eyes away from tanned, muscular legs. "In here." She patted the tote.

"Got your key?" He grinned.

She nodded. "Got yours?"

"Of course. C'mon, Fuller, get a move on," he said, heading for the front door.

They walked side by side down the steeply sloping road. Tess wore her floppy, wide-brimmed straw hat. David was bare headed, which wasn't smart. The sun was high now, beating down on their heads, the heat reflecting up from the tarred surface underfoot. The water glittered blue between the trees.

"It'll probably be crowded but we can still have a swim and cool off," Tess said. "There's not much surf here, too sheltered. We should go across to Manly one day."

"Do you surf?"

"Not really. I have a boogie board and I love the beach."

"Me too."

"There's another beach I go to sometimes. Obelisk Beach on the western shore." She glanced up at him. "It's clothing optional."

An eyebrow lifted above the dark glasses and he smiled but said nothing.

"You should have a hat on," Tess said.

"I'm fine."

"I could have given you one, you should have said so. But you can buy one at the beach. Don't want to get sunstroke before your concert."

"I think I'll survive. Thanks, Tess."

"There's a hole in the ozone layer, don't forget. The sun's much stronger in Australia than anywhere else. Even with a tan you can be burned to a crisp in no time. Skin cancer is . . ."

"Tess!"

"What?"

"Shut up."

"Sorry." He didn't return her smile. He strode down the hill beside her with his mouth a firm line.

"Very pretty." David said as they stood waiting to cross the road to the wide strip of parkland that lay between them and the sand. There were actually two beaches separated by a little jutting island connected to the shore by an arching, ornamental stone bridge. With very high tides or storms the water rushed underneath but at the moment the golden sand was dry.

The closest beach was longer but had yellow buoys marking off the area around a large stormwater pipe outlet. Moored yachts bobbed on the sparkling water. They crossed the road and walked across the grass, past the rotunda and the statue of the dog toward the old bathing pavilion, now a restaurant with a spectacular view of the far distant Heads, gateway to the ocean. This beach was small and the fact that it was in the harbor rather than facing the wild, open Pacific meant the waves were minimal and made it safer for swimmers. The shark net was still a necessity.

The land curved around on both sides, nestling the sand in a small east-facing cove. The sun shone; the breezed danced across the water and rustled the treetops. Many families enjoyed the safety of the secluded little beach. Tess left the promenade and guided David down the old-fashioned steps to a less-crowded patch of sand near the rocks on the northern end where she dumped the tote bag and her towel. David spread his towel neatly and kicked off his sandals. He pulled the T-shirt off over his head, folded it, and placed it on the towel.

Tess eyed his bare back as he bent down. "Like me to put sunscreen on your back?" She tried to sound casually helpful rather than a girl anxious to get her hands on him.

He straightened and turned giving her a full view of that chest and tanned flat stomach. "Thanks. Want me to do yours?"

"Yes, please!" She scrabbled about in the tote. When she turned he'd removed the shorts and stood before her in a pair of navy swim trunks. Not the Speedo variety, more like shorts but they showed plenty of muscled thigh.

"Turn around," she croaked.

"Hang on." He reached out and took the plastic bottle from her nerveless hand. He squeezed some cream into his palm and smiled. "I'll do the front while you do the back." He thrust the bottle into her hand.

"All right."

Tess held her breath and rubbed sticky white cream into the warm skin. Would he think she was peculiar if she rubbed her cheek over his back? She ran her fingers down the bumps of his spine and spread her palms out to feel the width of his rib cage and the muscles of his shoulders.

"Finished yet?" He ran his hands up and down his arms.

"Yes." She whipped off her tank top and dropped her shorts. She'd deliberately worn the white bikini because it showed off her figure very nicely. He didn't seem to notice.

"Turn around." He picked up the bottle she'd tossed onto his towel.

His hands were firm and purposeful working their way down from shoulders to waist. He'd be conscientiously covering every centimeter, not lingering, not fooling about, thinking purely of sun protection instead of having fantasies the way she had. She sighed. What turned him on?

The fingers left her body. "Done."

Not Tess Fuller, apparently.

"Race you," she called and sprinted toward the water, yelping as her bare feet connected with hot sand.

David pounded after her and they reached the incoming wavelets together, splashing and laughing and wading to deeper water.

Tess went back to the beach first. She sat on her towel watching him stroking along strongly, parallel to the shore. He swam well and obviously enjoyed the water. Another point in her favor. The house was so close it was like having their own private beach. At this time of day on a Saturday it was crowded but there were many other times when it was empty. A smile stretched her lips and she lay down pulling her hat over her face against the searing heat of the sun. The flirting had been a surprise. Maybe he just needed a nudge in the right direction.

David stood up and wiped his palms over his face, flicking wet hair from his eyes. What a good idea! Tess was right. He had woken up. Nothing so refreshing as a burst of saltwater still chilly from the winter currents. Wonderful. And so close to the house. Literally a ten-minute walk. He could start every day with a run and a quick swim. Were any of the apartments he was viewing near a beach? No. Pity. Still, if he found what he was looking for it wouldn't matter.

He waded ashore. Tess was flat on her back displaying that perfect body for all to see. Never again would he volunteer to apply her sunscreen or allow her to apply his. The physical explosion in his nerve center was almost catastrophic. Did she know what she was doing massaging his back that way? Probably. But she wouldn't think anything of it. To her, men were fair game, playthings. Girls like Tess grew bored with men like David very swiftly. Not exciting enough beyond an initial flirtatious dance just to prove they had the power. Attractive party girls couldn't help themselves. California had been full of them. Marianne.

"Where to first?"

David studied the page he'd cut from the paper. "Naremburn. There are two in the same block."

Tess accelerated and the Diva responded with an enthusiastic burst of speed. The piece of paper was nearly ripped from his hand by the slipstream so he folded it and stuffed it under his thigh for safekeeping. Tess laughed. "Woohoo," she cried. "I love this car."

David had to smile. She was like a five-year-old with an exciting new toy. A five-year-old with exceptional taste and the body of a fully grown goddess. She leaned forward and switched on the stereo system. He braced himself for another barrage from the Stones but instead a glorious tenor voice burst forth with an aria from Tosca.

She cast him a sideways glance as they paused briefly at a Stop sign. A sly, cheeky little smile lurked on her lips. Her eyes were hidden by the dark glasses. He hid his own smile by turning to look to the left in case she hadn't bothered to check for oncoming traffic.

That the first apartment was unsuitable became immediately apparent. With the greatest restraint Tess kept her opinion of the tiny cramped bedrooms and viewless windows to herself. David threw her a wide-eyed grimace that spoke volumes. The second place, a ground floor on a major thoroughfare right next to traffic lights received the most cursory of inspections. The third, in nearby Artarmon, seemed good from the street but once inside obviously needed severe renovations. Preferably involving a sledgehammer.

"It's moldy," stated Tess, peering into the dingy bathroom and emerging with a wrinkled nose. "Yucko. Chronic mold. You'd end up with athlete's foot and a lung condition."

Sitting in the car after the fifth and final dismal viewing for the afternoon David finally and reluctantly admitted she'd been right.

"You'll find somewhere better if you up the rent you're prepared to pay," she said. "I went into this thoroughly before I decided what to charge."

David sighed. "I don't want to pay more than three thirty."

"Keep looking," she said. "Something may turn up." But it wouldn't. Nothing would outdo what she was offering. Perhaps a little incentive would ease his decision. She started the engine. The Diva purred. No way was she defaulting on her payments and losing this treasure. "What if I knock twenty off my rent?" she said casually. She checked the rearview mirror, looked over her shoulder, and pulled into the traffic.

He didn't reply. Marcelo Alvarez started in on *Nessun Dorma.* How she loved Italian tenors! Except Marcelo was Argentinean. Glorious voice. Say something, David. She swung the Diva left sharply onto Military Road. Stop, start, stop, start in the late-afternoon traffic. What was David thinking? How to politely decline her offer?

"Well?" she demanded when his silence had extended beyond polite into annoying.

"Well what?"

"Three hundred a week."

He drew in a deep breath. "Thanks, Tess, but I don't think we should live together. Not on a long-term basis."

"Why not?"

"We're too different. We have to work together and we'd drive each other insane. I think we'd end up hating each other. We've both already said we don't want to share. You're only doing it out of necessity and so am I at the moment."

"That's ridiculous!"

"Why?"

"Because I need the rent and you need somewhere to live and my house is perfect. And I couldn't hate you," she added.

Silence again. Painful with the embarrassment of the unspoken.

She turned left and then right into their street. He still hadn't replied.

"But you could hate me," she said for him. Terse with the hurt. What did she have to do to gain his approval?

"Tess," he said softly but he didn't contradict her. She clicked the remote for the garage door and drove straight in. She refused to look at him, turned the engine off, and removed the key.

He held her bare arm lightly. His fingers burned into her skin. "Thanks for driving me about."

She pulled away and opened the door. "That's all right."

David got out and waited for her to come around the front of the car. "I just think we're very different, Tess," he said gently. "You're vivacious and messy and I'm quiet, neat, and a bit of an introvert. A perfectionist."

Her throat clogged. He stood looking down into her eyes with a soft, gentle expression. He smelled nice. Something with a mild citrus overtone. Yummy. Made her want to snuggle against his body. "I can be quiet too," she whispered. "And tidy."

He smiled and suddenly his lips brushed her cheek. For a moment his cheek rested against hers, warm and slightly rough with stubble. She edged closer, breathing in the scent of him, eyes closed, body craving the feel of him.

"This isn't a good idea, Tess," he murmured in a quite different voice. She whipped her arms from around his neck where they'd somehow landed, and straightened with a jerk. His face was very close, her eyes fastened on his lips. Kiss him. Properly. Make him see what staying here could mean.

He patted her shoulder. Just like Daddy.

Chapter Four

David backed Tess' Mercedes convertible carefully down the driveway. "I hope you know what you're doing," he said, "letting me drive."

"I hope *you* know what *you're* doing," she retorted cheerily.

She'd bounced back incredibly quickly from that misunderstanding yesterday. Fortunately. He wasn't good with emotional women. He paused at the street to check both ways. What a treat, driving this car. She was very generous even after he'd resisted her thinly veiled advance. It had taken all his self-control but he wasn't letting on how close he'd come to kissing her on the bonnet of the Diva.

"Left," she said.

"Right," he muttered, concentrating on the gear configuration before launching them into traffic. Arm's length for Tess. Old friends. Buddies.

"No, left. And stay on the left side of the road."

He glanced at her. She was wearing her lovely broad smile. "Very funny, Fuller." He swung into the street, changed gears, and the Merc roared off like a rocket. "Wow! Fantastic."

"I know." Tess laughed in delight. Her hair blew around her face in wild confusion but she didn't seem fussed. A style like hers looked wild all the time. Suited her perfectly. He'd absolutely done the right thing by not responding. Now she'd know he wasn't interested and she'd move on to someone else. He slowed at an intersection. "Go straight on and take the next right." Except he was interested. To the point of danger. But he hadn't gotten to where he was today by indulging himself in fleeting and potentially disastrous passions.

The Merc handled superbly. He began to relax, comfortable with the gearshift and the response of the steering. "Great car, Tess." It even took his attention away from her legs, which were distractingly displayed next to him from under the hem of her sundress.

"Told you."

"I never doubted you."

"I wouldn't spend all that money on a dud. I did my research. I do know a few things."

"Tess," he said sharply. "You don't have to convince me of anything. I'm not your brother. As far as I'm concerned, you're a woman with very good taste in cars. Your personal finances are not my business—or anyone else's."

"All right."

She directed him to an address in Lane Cove, another harborside suburb on the same side of the bridge but farther west. Cars lined both sides of the street for a block in either direction. "Go back and park in the driveway," said Tess. "You're the guest of honor."

David circled the block and did as she suggested. "I'll tell the hosts you made me do it." He pulled on the hand brake.

"They'll know that." She flung the door open and stepped out before he could come around and open it for her. He handed her the car keys instead. She grinned and dropped them into the little silk Chinese embroidered bag slung over her bare shoulder. Honey gold skin glowed above and below her white dress, strappy high-heeled sandals and ruby red toenails. Tousled lion's mane of hair that she poked at with her fingers. "Do I look all right?"

He studied her critically. Did she look all right or what? She was stunning. His lips tingled at the memory of her skin, her perfume warm from her body. "Yep. Do I?"

That wide smile. "Yep." She opened the car door again. "Mustn't forget the wine." She straightened, brandishing the bottle from her father's well-stocked wine cellar. Something she'd casually shown him when he suggested they bring a bottle to the party. "Let's go."

As they ascended the steps to the house she said, "Watch out for Yvonne, Stan's wife."

A roar of voices and music came from inside. The front door was on the latch but they'd barely stepped over the threshold before a lemon-yellow-clad woman pounced. "David Montgomery! Tess, hello. Welcome." She clutched his hand. "We're so excited to have you here. I'm Yvonne Mazur."

"How do you do, Yvonne. Thank you for inviting me."

All teeth and wide red mouth in a lightly freckled middle-aged face topped with platinum blond hair. "Stan's in the garden. Come with me."

He turned to Tess who was grinning. She gave a little wave as Yvonne clasped David's arm and dragged him, a helpless captive, into the crowd of people. Friendly faces smiled and said hello as they passed. He did his best to acknowledge the greetings searching for those faces he'd recognize from last night's dinner. Saw none. These were the musos, not the bosses. They plowed through the living room and family room, across a terrace, and came to rest in the garden. Not as large as Tess' but lovely all the same with a wide expanse of lawn packed with people, and a breathtaking view of the water.

"Here he is at last." Yvonne presented him to a slim, pale-skinned, dark-haired man with a receding hairline who stood chatting to Ian. "David, this is my husband

Stan. He's first desk with you." Stan gave a stiff little European-style bow and clasped David's hand.

"How very pleased we are to have you in the City. Welcome, David."

"Thank you very much, Stan. You've no idea how proud I am to be given this opportunity."

"Hello there. Some of us were getting worried," Ian said.

"Why?" Ian always looked worried as far as David could judge from such a short acquaintance. A waiter offered a tray of drinks. David took juice. He'd forgotten to check with Tess who was the designated driver. She had the keys; she owned the car. It was his welcome party. It must be her. Not that he planned on getting drunk but if he was driving he wouldn't drink at all. But could she be trusted? Party Girl.

Yvonne leaned closer, still gripping his arm in an unpleasantly familiar manner. "Ian means me. I was worried. Tess isn't exactly reliable."

"Really?"

"That's not strictly accurate," murmured Ian. "She's always on time to rehearsals and concerts. Never missed a thing connected with the orchestra and her job."

Yvonne ignored him. Her eyes were unpleasantly intense, pale blue. "She's very scatterbrained. Never had to take responsibility for anything. I told Stan you could have stayed here with us when your flat fell through. You still can." Her mouth reminded him of a big, overblown tropical flower—wide, red, and fleshy. The type that fed on insects.

"I'm quite comfortable with Tess for the moment, thanks, Yvonne. Kind of you to offer though." He sipped juice and gazed around the garden.

"Tess has a marvelous house, doesn't she?" said Ian hastily. "I thought you'd be comfortable there in the interim."

"It's perfect, thank you." Thank goodness for the change of tack. He wasn't up to fabricating excuses for not staying with this overbearing woman. Tess may have her faults but she wasn't a gossip. "The music room is superb. Tess said her father had it engineered specially for her."

"Her father was Lionel Fuller." Yvonne emphasized the name with raised eyebrows. "I suppose she told you. Modesty isn't one of our Tess' failings."

"Tess and I were at the music school in Canberra together," said David evenly. He stretched the truth ever so slightly. "I've known her for a long time." He gave Yvonne a little smile hoping to staunch the flow of vitriol before the tongue got really revved up.

"Well, you'd know perfectly well then, Tess never wants for anything and if she wants something, she gets it. And don't we all know all about that!" This last was accompanied by a meaningful raise of two penciled-in eyebrows. They looked like worms.

"Yvonne," said Stan, frowning. Ian shifted uncomfortably from one foot to the other but Yvonne was not to be deflected from her goal, which appeared to be warning David of Tess' evil intentions.

"David must know what I mean. She's a man trap. She won't have changed a bit. That sort of girl never does. Everyone in the orchestra knows about Raoul. At least David will have his defenses up. Forewarned is forearmed."

"That's enough, Yvonne," said Stan. "We must mingle. Excuse us, please." He grasped his wife firmly by the arm, nodded to David and Ian, and marched her away.

"My defenses?" asked David. What was Tess? A missile? A man-seeking missile? Apart from that one little flirtatious gesture she hadn't shown any particular interest in him except for the freely admitted teenage crush. And he'd invited that embrace by kissing her. She was generous and friendly to a fault.

Ian grimaced and hissed air through his teeth. "I suppose I should fill you in—you'll hear it through the grapevine soon enough."

"You don't have to tell me anything. I hate gossip."

"It's probably best you know. It does affect the orchestra and it'll save any umm . . . awkwardness."

David nodded reluctantly.

Ian swallowed some of his red wine. "Last year Tess had a thing with one of the cellists."

"A thing?" His heart sagged.

Ian licked his lips and gazed over David's shoulder. "A relationship. Raoul Cesari. Problem was, he was a real ladies' man and when they broke up, as they inevitably did, given Raoul's reputation, things became very . . . shall we say messy. He was furious, she was furious and very hurt. Tess isn't good at hiding her feelings. He accused her of all sorts of things, not least stringing him along and being little Miss Spoiled Rich Girl."

"Was she stringing him along? Was the breakup—the mess—Tess' fault?" An icy torrent of shock flooded his body. He glanced around the crowded garden but couldn't see the wild mane of hair. Was she working on someone else right now? Smiling, flirting, and flashing those gorgeous eyes with all that tanned skin on display. Playing with someone's feelings?

"Raoul was hardly innocent," said Ian. "In another era he would have been what was known as a cad. You know, for all her craziness, Tess is a bit of a lost child when it comes to some things."

David looked at Ian with renewed interest. What things? "You think it was entirely his fault?"

"Raoul was the sort of person a few people think Tess is. She's not manipulative and calculating, or cruel. She's not greedy. He was. She's passionate and impulsive but very kindhearted. In many ways vulnerable. He definitely took advantage of her."

"But most people think Tess was at fault. Why?"

"Not everyone. Of those who took sides at all, the women tended to line up with Raoul. Heaven knows why. Jealousy perhaps, that he hadn't chosen them? Who knows how female brains work. Tess didn't make herself very popular by not saying anything constructive either about him or in her own defense. Unfortunately that left the field wide open for Raoul's version plus speculation." He gave a little half snort of laughter. "She threw her shoe at him once after a rehearsal."

"Good heavens! Is Raoul still with the City?"

"No. He accepted a position in Hong Kong."

"But Tess stayed."

Ian nodded. "She pretends it meant nothing but it's a difficult thing for her to live down. She was very hurt by the whole affair. Humiliating to have the breakup of one's relationship played out in public. Raoul made sure everyone knew his side of things."

David shook his head. "Incredible."

"Not really. Surely you've come across this sort of thing before?"

"Yes, of course, but I don't get involved. I try to distance myself." Especially if shoe throwing was likely.

It's not the first time work colleagues have had an affair," said Ian mildly. "Happens all the time, especially in a hothouse situation like ours. Eighty talented, artistic, emotional, expressive people struggling to create beautiful music in sometimes pressure situations . . . what can you expect?"

"I expect people to respect each other for a start," said David. "And I expect people to keep their private lives private and not use the orchestra as a stage for their dramas."

Ian smiled. "In a perfect world."

David sensed a measure of disapproval. Surely he

didn't condone such behavior? Brawling in public. It wouldn't do the orchestra's reputation much good, especially if the press got wind of a juicy story like that. Lionel Fuller's daughter must be worth a column or two in the trashy mags.

Ian nodded toward the buffet table. "Come and have something to eat."

Tess lost sight of David almost immediately but she did find Grace, heavily pregnant and sitting on a chair chatting to Eric.

"Hello, Tess."

"Hi."

"How's our fearless new leader?" asked Eric.

"I heard him practicing. He's wonderful. I'll introduce you if I can find him." She looked around helplessly. "Yvonne got him as soon as we set foot in the house."

"That's that then, he'll be a gibbering mess by now," said Eric. "Drink, Tess?"

"I brought this." She handed him the wine. "But I'd like juice please. I think I'm driving."

"From Pa's cellar?" Eric read the label. "Excellent!" He disappeared with her bottle. Tess sat beside Grace. "Did your friend ever say why she didn't want to share the house?"

Grace smiled and looked away to where someone had burst into raucous laughter. "Ummm." Grace was such a sweetie she hated upsetting anyone. Her gaze returned to Tess. "She really liked you. And loved the house of course. It was just . . ."

"Hannibal," supplied Tess. "He's got gas problems, poor old boy."

"I know! Old dogs do that. Woof's the same but we all adore him so we put up with it."

Tess frowned. "David said that was why I couldn't find someone."

"Does he mind?"

"He grumbles but he hasn't actually said anything really bad. He makes jokes about gas masks."

Grace laughed. "That's good."

"Do you think so? He doesn't like dogs much but he's taken Fid out for a walk so he may be softening."

"Here, Tess." Eric handed her a glass of red. He had one of his own. "This is a terrific drop. Sorry, Grace, no booze for you."

"That's all right, the smell makes me feel sick anyway. Could you get me something to eat, please?"

"I won't drink either thanks, Eric," said Tess again. He must have been so taken with the wine label his ears switched off. "I'm driving."

"I'll just have to drink it myself." He placed the second glass carefully by his chair and went away for Tess' juice

A few minutes later David and Ian threaded their way through the crowd heading toward the food-laden table. Tess stood with her plate in the queue behind Eric, watching David meeting his new colleagues. Most had heard of him, many were die-hard cynics and would wait for him to prove his worth. Too young had been the consensus. Oscar, who had retired from the position, had been Leader for twenty-two years. It was a big chair to fill. Everyone loved Oscar and most had expected Stan to move into first chair. Yvonne, of course, had not hidden her opinion of who was best qualified.

Tess served herself salad and barbecued fish. David moved away with Ian and stood talking to three double bass players. She edged into the group.

"Hi, everyone. Excuse me. David?" He turned to her with a such a cool face she almost retreated in confusion. "Umm, I . . . I'd like you to umm . . . to meet some people," she stuttered. "When you've got a minute." He nodded imperceptibly and turned back to Steve. "Over there," she said. "In the corner. The pregnant girl. Grace."

"Sure." And he virtually turned his back on her. Tess retired with the disapproving eyes of Sarah and John boring into her back. They'd never forgiven her for falling in love with the wrong man, the self-righteous creeps. No doubt they were busily filling David in on the whole sorry affair with Tess Fuller cast, as usual, in the role of mad, saint-slaying Salome.

"What's wrong?" asked Grace when Tess slumped into the chair beside her and Eric.

"I think David's getting the dirt on me from the bass section."

"It was bound to happen," said Eric. "If they didn't mention it Yvonne would."

"It shouldn't make any difference to him," said Grace. "He's an old friend, isn't he? That's what Ian says."

"We studied in Canberra together but he was two years ahead of me. He didn't socialize at all so I'd hardly say we were friends. He didn't even really remember me except by my grossly exaggerated reputation. I remembered him, though."

"Well you would, wouldn't you?" Grace sent her a little grin.

"Why?" Eric shoved a large forkful of potato salad into his mouth and looked from Grace to Tess in expectation.

Grace rolled her eyes. "You're a boy, you wouldn't understand." Grace and Eric really were old friends, going back many years through school and house sharing. They had an easy brother-sister-type relationship that Tess had never had with a man. Until two days ago when, a relationship being out of the question, the possibility emerged with David. Or so she'd imagined.

Tess said, "Does Harry know his pregnant wife scopes out other guys?"

"Harry trusts Eric to keep me under control."

Tess finished her lunch and put her plate on the floor by her chair. Grace and Harry were the ideal couple, totally besotted with each other after two years together, expecting their first child to go with Harry's son by his first wife. Happy, happy, happy. How did people do it? How did they find the right person in the roiling sea of wrong people?

She picked up the spare glass of red. Better not knock it over accidentally or there'd be hell to pay. Break a glass and stain the carpet all in one go. Yvonne would ban her for life.

Should she offer a glass of the red to David? Who was driving home? They hadn't discussed it but he'd probably expect her to. It was his party. He was still chatting to the bass players. She watched him nodding and smiling then suddenly he turned and caught her staring. His eyes locked with hers for an instant but someone walked between them and broke the beam. Unmistakably angry. Why? Shaken, she rejoined the Eric and Grace conversation and listened without understanding a word they said.

"Hello." All polished politeness. "I'm David Montgomery." Eric stood up and shook hands. Tess' heart thumped hard. He wasn't the same man who'd driven here, joking with her, laughing and enjoying her car.

"Eric Sinclair, trombone number two."

Tess said, "And this is Grace Birmingham in the first violins."

"Hello, Grace," David held out his hand accompanied by a charm-laden smile. "Don't get up. How long do you have to go?"

"Six weeks."

"She looks ready to pop, doesn't she?" asked Eric.

"I'm very excited about hearing you play the Beethoven on Thursday," said Grace. "Tess said you sound marvelous."

"Oh, thank you. A live broadcast is always nerve-racking. I'm looking forward to the rehearsal tomorrow, hearing the City." He glanced swiftly at Tess. "His eyes dropped to the glass in her hand. "Who's driving?"

"I will."

"But you're drinking."

Tess opened her mouth to correct him.

"That's only her first," interrupted Eric. "Bottle," he added with a laugh.

"Eric!" said Grace while Tess' horrified mind whirled.

Eric continued cheerily, "A glass with food wouldn't put anyone over the limit."

"Maybe not but I don't like taking chances," David said with icicles tinkling. "It was nice to meet you, Grace, Eric. I must move on. Excuse me." He slid away.

"What a total stinker," muttered Tess. Angry tears picked at her lids.

"Who me?" asked Eric.

"Him. Picking at me for drinking wine when I hadn't had a drop." Treating her like a child, humiliating her in front of Grace and Eric. "He didn't even give me a chance to tell him. Just assumed the worst."

"And you didn't help." Grace frowned at Eric.

"What did I do?" He sat down and resumed eating. "He's right. Drunk driving's not on."

"Where's the rest of that bottle, Eric?" Tess said. "If he thinks I'm already drinking I may as well be." She stood up. "Don't worry I won't drive, I'll catch a cab."

"Don't, Tess," said Grace sternly, catching her hand.

"Imagine how pleased Yvonne and the razor gang will be if David has to lug your senseless body home."

Tess glowered. What a horrendous image. "True. And I might say something I'll regret later. Probably would."

"Don't give them the satisfaction of being right." Eric stood up too and leaned close. A conspirator. "What would really upset them is if you drink water and smile sweetly and agree with everything."

"I'd explode. Or implode."

"But David would be impressed," said Grace. "And you *are* living together."

"Only for this week," said Tess glumly. "He thinks he'll find somewhere better and I even dropped the rent a bit to make him change his mind."

"All the more reason to be on best behavior," said Eric. "He's not going to consider staying on if you drink today. Drunken women are the pits, Tess. Ugly as sin."

"I know. I don't drink much anyway and never when I'm driving." Tess heaved a vast sigh. "I'm so hopeless . . . I decided to be a much better person this year. After . . . well you know. But it's really hard. I like socializing and I like men and they like me. What am I supposed to do?"

"Get thee to a nunnery?" suggested Eric.

"You know what Shakespeare meant by that, don't you?" asked Grace.

"I'm not that bad, am I?" cried Tess amid the laughter.

"Of course not. I reckon some of those dried-up old

prunes are, and were, jealous. They don't like anyone to have too good a time when they're not. The men wished they could have been in Raoul's place and the women wished he'd look at them. He did have impeccable taste though, I must say, despite being a cad of the highest order."

Tess' eyes filled with amazed tears as she listened to Eric's summation of the situation. He'd never told her how he felt before. He and Grace had never said anything much except to maintain their friendship along with a handful of others when many of her colleagues had turned their backs and muttered. She slid her arms around his waist and hugged him, hard.

"Thanks, Eric." He returned the hug.

"Anytime."

"What a pity we don't fancy each other," she said letting him go.

"I always thought that about Eric and me too," said Grace. "But then Harry came along and I realized what was missing."

"Thanks a lot, ladies." Eric gave a half bow. "I'm so glad to be the permanent back stop. A nice guy. The kiss of death."

"Stop complaining. You've got plenty of girlfriends," said Grace.

"That's right and I have a hot date with one of them tonight."

Tess smiled absently as Grace began requesting details of Eric's new amour. David was over in the corner talking to Viktor now. He didn't concern himself with gossip and innuendo. All Viktor cared about was the orchestra and the dedication of his players. Outside of that his primary concern was his wife and two small children. Another happy couple. How depressing it all was.

Tess excused herself and wandered outside into the garden. She chatted here and there to various people. Now that Raoul had gone, much of the tension and awkwardness had gone with him. People's attention moved on to other things and Tess was accepted again. Though not fully. She knew by the way some people looked at her they hadn't forgotten and would never condone her behavior. Throwing things . . . not a good look, she had to admit. David obviously fell into that camp. He'd be horrified by such a physical display of emotion. His old manner hadn't changed—distancing himself and this time without even hearing her side of the story.

She looked at her watch. Nearly four. She wanted to go home. All her enjoyment of the occasion fled when David chided her. Why did he have such a strong effect on her? Why did she crave his approval? He was right about their differences—she loved company; he was the musical equivalent of a computer nerd. Somehow he'd robbed her of the pleasure of this party.

He stood on the terrace with Yvonne now. They were looking straight at her. She raised her glass of tropical juice toward them in a toast and drained the contents in one long swallow. Let them think it was vodka and orange. Let them think what they liked. She placed the empty tumbler on the tray of a passing waiter and headed for the steps to join them.

"It really is a most lovely party, thank you very much for going to all this trouble for us, Yvonne." She gave them both the benefit of her best social smile. Not for nothing had she been brought up in the most exclusive circles. She could turn it on when necessary. Charm and manners fit for a palace.

Yvonne blinked in surprise. She glanced at David, whose eyes had narrowed in suspicion, and fluttered a hand heavy with clunky, gem-laden rings.

"It was nothing. A pleasure. David deserved a welcome and no one else seemed to think of it. Or really, has the facilities. Except you, Tess." She stopped as the implication of her words appeared to sink through the thatch of bouffant hair to what passed as a brain. That Tess wouldn't think of anything other than herself.

"Thank you, Yvonne," David said quickly. "It was very generous of you and Stan. I've enjoyed meeting everyone very much. It was a lovely idea."

Tess maintained her smile even though her fingers briefly curled into a fist. She turned and met his gaze with the perfect amount of polite concern. "David, I'm heading home. If you'd like to stay on I'm sure someone can drop you or perhaps you could take a taxi."

He licked his lips. "Are you all right to drive?"

"You mustn't drive, Tess. You've been drinking," piped up the lovely hostess.

Tess looked Yvonne directly in her washed-out blue

eyes. "No matter what you may think of me, I don't drink and drive. I've had no alcohol at all. I've drunk water and juice. Thanks, Yvonne. I'll see myself out." She turned to David. "I'll see you later. Good-bye." He didn't flinch but the steady gaze made her turn away before she said something less well mannered.

"Good-bye," trilled Yvonne. There was undeniable relief in her voice and she added before Tess was out of earshot, "No need for you to leave, David."

Tess came across Stan on her way to the front door. "Leaving already?" he asked.

"Yes. I have the dogs to feed and Fid needs a walk. Thanks for the party."

He leaned in and kissed her cheek with real affection, giving her shoulders a little squeeze. He'd been one of her staunchest allies. Calm and accepting. A good friend.

"Take care."

She fluttered her fingers in an Yvonne-esque wave and escaped. The Diva sat in the street reflecting sunlight from all her polished silver and chrome surfaces. Boy, would she like a drive somewhere! Fast. On a road where she could let the Diva free. Get away from everything. Maybe the freeway north to Newcastle. That was closest. Blow away the embarrassment, the hurt. Forget the condemnation and judgment in David's eyes. Go.

Tess headed north and forty minutes later, ensconced in the outside lane with the late-afternoon sun warming her face and the wind tugging at her hair, she let the Diva rip.

The front of the house was in darkness when she returned. The Diva's lights swept the driveway and the gate where Fid should have been waiting anxiously for his dinner. She was late, shivering in the evening cool. The poor boy had probably given up and gone to bed. Hannibal would be asleep for sure. Where was David? Had he stayed on and been invited to someone else's for dinner? Had he decided to take up Yvonne's offer and move in with her and Stan? It wouldn't surprise her if he had. He and Yvonne operated on a similar wavelength.

The roller door slid securely into place behind the Diva. Tess stepped out of the garage and the rear sensor light came on, illuminating the path to the back door. Fid didn't come running. Her breath quickened. He must be inside. With David. The back door was locked. No sounds came from anywhere. She went round to the front door just in case. How many times had she come home like this as a teenager? The same guilty feeling, her father waiting inside to tear strips off her. Preparing a defiant, brazen face. Determined not to make excuses.

Ridiculous! This was her house, she was a grown woman beholden to no one, especially not a pious, self-righteous . . . The alarm was off. David was home. Fid scampered up the hall to meet her, stumpy tail wagging frantically.

She patted the wiggling body. "Are you hungry? Me too. Give me five minutes." First stop bathroom and bedroom to change into warmer track pants and long-sleeved sweatshirt. Her hair was a mess. She dragged a brush through it. Fid sat watching. "Right." Now to face the dragon.

The television was on but the sound was muted for ads. David sat on the couch. He glanced at her but said nothing. Tess moved stiff with apprehension to the kitchen and opened the fridge. Fid sat hopefully at her feet.

"They've had their dinner. Hannibal was already in bed. I heard him snuffling so I left his food in his dish. I fed Fid in the laundry room so he wouldn't eat Hannibal's." The voice was mild, unperturbed.

"Oh. Thanks." The stiffness melted away in relief. She closed the fridge door. "Fibber," she said to Fid. He waggled his bottom and licked his lips, grinning.

She inspected the cupboard for something edible. Lucky they'd been shopping this morning. There were two types of canned soup to choose from and a fresh loaf of Italian bread. "Like some celery soup?" she called. He had no right to judge her. Was he?

"Yes, please." He switched the TV off and got up. "I was worried about you," he said accusingly.

Uh-oh. Here it came. "Why?" She concentrated on the tin opener and the soup. He sounded like her father, until he'd given up wondering or caring what she was doing—when she was about sixteen.

"I thought you were going home."

"So? I changed my mind." She dumped the soup into a saucepan and flung the pan onto the gas.

"You could have rung."

"Why should I?" Tess grabbed a spoon and stirred in water. "This is exactly why I hate sharing. Although no housemates I've ever had cared where I was and vice versa. And I certainly didn't have to clock in with any of them!"

He shrugged. "You might've had an accident. You seemed upset when you left, that's all." He leaned against the bench.

And why would that have been? "Did I?"

"Yes. I would've come with you but you left too fast."

Tess stopped stirring. "Even though I was drunk?" she demanded.

"You weren't."

"But you thought I might be, didn't you? Irresponsible Tess," she said bitterly. "You don't even know me, yet that's what you assume based on what you remember from years ago and what gossips like Yvonne told you."

"I prefer to make up my own mind about people. You said you hadn't been drinking. I believed you." He came around the bench and took the spoon from her hand. "This will stick unless you keep stirring."

Tess wiped a hand across her eyes. Stupid tears. "What you said was really insulting. In front of my friends."

"I'm sorry. I was wrong."

"You sounded like my father."

He studied her, still stirring the soup. "I thought he doted on you."

"He did but he treated me as if I was seven years old. His darling little girl. He never took me seriously."

"Where's your mother?"

"She cleared out when we I was nine. She ran off with some rich Brazilian and then moved on to a Frenchman and then a Texan and as far as I know she's in Dallas. Or Houston. Somewhere." She shrugged.

"Make some toast," said David. "Your father never remarried?"

"No. He said he'd learned his lesson with my mother. Women were good for pleasure but not to be given any sort of responsibility."

"Toast," prompted David. He turned off the gas under the soup and took two bowls from the cupboard.

Tess sliced bread and started the toaster. She handed him a ladle.

"What sort of soup is this, did you say?" he asked.

"Celery."

He pulled a face. "Got any Tabasco?"

"Yes."

She buttered toast while David ladled soup into the bowls. They carried them carefully to the table along with the plate of toast.

"Were you really worried?" she asked.

"Only that you might have wrecked the Diva."

Tess broke off small pieces of toast and dropped them

into her soup. "Yvonne told you about Raoul, didn't she?"

He swallowed a mouthful. "No. Ian did and then Sarah and John gave me a different version."

"And?" She poked at the floating croutons with her spoon.

"And what?"

"You think I'm a girl who plays around and breaks men's hearts deliberately."

He continued to spoon up mouthfuls. Scoop, sip, swallow. Scoop, sip, swallow. He didn't have to say a word. She knew exactly what he was thinking. She gritted her teeth.

He put his spoon down and took a piece of toast. "What you do or have done is none of my business," he said quietly.

"But you must have an opinion," she cried.

He raised his eyes to hers. "I don't think you want to hear it."

"You self-righteous . . . ," she hissed. "You haven't even heard my side."

"Go on then. Tell me." He bit into the crunchy, hard crust of the toasted Italian bread. Crumbs dropped to the table but he didn't move to clear them.

"No." Tess leaned back in her chair. Her soup was untouched. Her appetite gone. "There's no point. You already think you know what I'm like and you've decided I messed Raoul around—probably just for fun."

David stared at his bowl. A muscle tightened in his

jaw. He resumed eating. Tess waited for a response, a reply. Anything. He took another piece of toast, dipped it in the soup, and chewed studiously without looking at her. He swallowed. "By the way, your brother rang again. Didn't you call him back?"

Tess shook her head. Her stomach gurgled. His mildness took the edge off her anger. He really didn't want to know about the dismal affair. Her appetite crashed back. She spooned up soup.

David continued, "He wanted to know why your mobile is permanently switched off. Is it?"

Tess nodded and swallowed.

"I think he thinks I've got you tied up in the cellar." Was that an attempt at humor? His way of smoothing over their rift? Or didn't he think there'd been a rift and she was just being hysterical?

"There's no cellar."

"He's beginning to sound suspicious. You'd better call him."

"I will."

"Why is your mobile off?"

"So I don't have to answer it."

"Fair enough."

Tess scraped the last of the soup from her bowl. She'd better ring Stu before he really started asking awkward questions. Was David's indifference better or worse than his unstated and presumably unfavorable opinion?

Chapter Five

"How long is your friend staying?" asked Stuart when Tess called him. "You know you need my approval for anything more than a few weeks' visit."

"I know, I know. A week," said Tess. "Maybe longer. He's looking for somewhere of his own. But it's hard. He's performing on Thursday night so I don't want him to worry until that's over. He's a fantastic player, Stu. It's his debut with us."

"I'm coming to Sydney on Wednesday for some meetings so I'd like to stay from then until Friday. Is that all right?"

"Of course."

Cripes! Pleasure at seeing her big brother was dashed by a sudden and terrible thought. He'd see the Diva.

"I'll come to the concert. The Japanese guys I'm meeting will love it."

"Okay. You'll have to let Ian know."

"Yep, I'll have Joanne organize it tomorrow."

Tess hung up with a whole new dread in her stomach. Stu would want to know where the Diva came from. He'd ask questions. That's what he did. He was brilliant at it. And he'd want proper answers.

David was stacking the dishwasher when Tess came out of the study with the phone clutched in white-knuckled fingers.

"Stu's coming to stay on Wednesday," she said. "He has business in Sydney."

He smiled at her with a soup bowl in his hand. "That's good."

"No it's not."

He straightened. "Why?"

"He'll see the Diva."

"He'll be impressed."

"No, no, no, he won't." Tess replaced the phone on its stand, shaking her head, her brow furrowed with the dread of it all. "He'll be horrified. He'll want to know how I can afford her."

"Tell him." He dumped the spoons and buttering knife into the basket, separating them into like with like.

"No . . . it's . . . it's complicated." She turned the silver ring on her middle finger round and round. "Can I say she's yours?"

"Mine? No!" Outrage. She might've known David

would be no help in a situation like this. May as well ask a nun—or rather, a priest.

"He'll only be here for two days, he'll never know it's not true."

"*I* will, Tess. Look I've no idea what you're up to or why this should be such an issue but I am *not* becoming involved." The toast plate went into the rack with a decisive clunk.

"Please?"

"No."

The way he was glaring at her made it quite clear he wasn't changing his mind. He shook his head and sighed. "If you must, tell him you're garaging it for a friend."

"Brilliant!" She shot both arms in the air and did a little dance of joy. "Yes!" If he wasn't so obviously annoyed with her she'd kiss him. "Why didn't I think of that?"

David closed the dishwasher and picked up the pink sponge to wipe down the stovetop. Tess was hopeless. Beautiful and almost irresistibly desirable but hopeless. She went from devastation to elation in the blink of an eye, from anger to calm in the time it took to swallow a mouthful of soup. Her smile dazzled him. When she looked at him the way she looked now, eyes sparkling, body vibrant with delight, dancing about like a child, he forgot everything he knew about her, everything he'd been told about her. She made his heart beat faster, his blood flow fuller, his energy seem boundless. He wanted to be near her. Forever.

But she gave her love to anyone, any man who asked, it seemed, according to Yvonne. His heart couldn't be on offer to a girl like that. He couldn't expose his desire to her for an instant. If she had the slightest inkling how he felt . . . Raoul—the name curled in his mind like a serpent.

"Are you frightened of your brother?" He gave the stove one last wipe and turned to the bench top where she'd spread a layer of crumbs. "Put the bread away."

Tess did as she was told but didn't answer his question.

"Why can't you just tell him about the Diva? You're an adult, you have a good job. What's the problem?"

"I told you! He'll be angry because he'll think I'm being too extravagant and he'll go on and on about my wasteful ways and how irresponsible I am. He can be a real pain when he wants to be."

She was hiding something. David watched her as she turned away flicking her fingers at Fid to take him outside. No point pushing her. It wasn't his business anyway. But it was odd. Tess was usually quite open, disarmingly and disconcertingly so.

When she returned she said, "Stu is bringing his Japanese business cronies to the concert."

"Really. That's nice of him."

"Yes and no. Stu's company is a sponsor. He can have tickets whenever he wants. He likes to impress his clients with culture."

"I'm looking forward to meeting him."

"Mmm. Feel like coffee?"

Quick change of subject. What was it with her and her brother?

"Nervous?" Tess glanced at David sitting silently beside her as the Diva idled at a red light. Much more somber atmosphere this Monday morning. No music on the stereo and even the day was cooler with the sun hidden behind huge puffy boulders of white-gray, and rain forecast for later.

"Yes," he admitted with a tight little smile. "It's always hard starting with a new orchestra."

"But everyone's met you already and we're predisposed to like you," Tess said, knowing it was scant comfort. When the performance terrors struck, words weren't much use. The light changed and she moved sedately across the intersection. She'd put the top up before they left this morning. The last thing she wanted was to physically terrorize him before his first rehearsal.

He sat there like a coiled spring. His hands moved constantly, rubbing against each other, fiddling with his shirt cuffs, smoothing his hair. Maybe a death-defying career through the Sydney traffic would be just what he needed—take his mind off the impending debut.

"I threw up before my final exam recital," she said. "I'm much better now but I'm still pretty nervous before a concert."

"Mmm. I've never thrown up."

"Once we get started I'm fine. It's the anticipation."

"Yes, you'd think we'd become immune after this long but I'm not, I just control it better."

"Me too." Tess threw him a smile, catching his eye briefly before returning her attention to the traffic. Ten minutes later she pulled the Diva into the carpark closest to the rehearsal hall. David collected his music and violin from the rear seat, his movements jerky and awkward. Nerves did that, tightened the muscles and froze the nerve endings.

He waited for her to lock the car and walked stiff-legged beside her to the exit. "I'm glad you're with me today," he said abruptly. "Much easier to arrive with someone."

Tess tucked her free arm into his and squeezed gently before releasing him. His muscles were rock hard. "You'll be fine. You've done this a million times—well, almost."

"I know. It's just . . ." He stopped and looked down at her with a slightly creased brow as if deciding whether to share something, a secret. He started walking again and she walked beside him almost holding her breath, waiting, desperate not to spoil the moment with a wrong word, a miscalculated expression or gesture. "Leading the City has been a dream of mine since I was ten." He glanced at her, perhaps waiting for an explosion of derisive laughter or some wisecrack. She nodded, silent. Of course she understood a dream like that. He went on,

"They toured and did a concert in Wagga and my parents took us. Oscar Stevenson played the Beethoven."

She stopped dead. "And now *you* are," she said softly as the full realization of the importance to him of this day, this approaching moment, swamped her faculties and caused a momentary short circuit. "That's wonderful. Congratulations." And he'd shared with her, opened up a teensy bit. More than a teensy bit, he'd shared something very intimate and personal. A groundswell of emotion made her swallow a ridiculous desire to cry that he'd never understand and she'd never be able to explain.

He continued on a couple of paces before realizing she'd stopped. He turned, shifted his violin to his other hand. Some of the tension left his body as he studied her face. His eyes lingered on hers, on the lids heavy with unshed tears. She blinked again and one drop escaped. He stepped closer, reached out a gentle finger and wiped the tear away with a tiny smile. "Thanks, Fuller. No need to cry, though." His gaze entwined with hers and some connection was made, some deeper understanding she couldn't articulate.

Tess grinned, sniffed back more wayward salty moisture and strode on. "Better not be late on your first day. An angry Viktor is not a pretty sight."

"I'll tell him you were driving."

"Yep, that's right," she said with a short, resigned laugh. "Blame me. Everyone else does."

"No! Don't put yourself down." The vehemence

brought her up short. "I was joking, Tess. Not a very good joke, I'm sorry, but I don't blame you for anything. You mustn't think that."

Tess stared, her mouth partway open in surprise. She swallowed, wet her lips with her tongue. "No, I know." It came out as the merest whisper. She cleared her throat, fired up her voice, smiled. "Thanks but you don't know me very well yet."

"I'm learning." For an instant that deeper connection sparked once more. Then he jerked his head in the direction of the exit. "Come on."

David played sublimely, of course, and during the break after they'd finished rehearsing Beethoven he was surrounded by adoring violinists from his new section. Tess sipped tea with Eric and watched the adulation from a corner of the recreation room.

"He's very good." Eric dunked a biscuit, which immediately dissolved into a soggy mess. He proceeded to rescue it with a teaspoon.

"That's disgusting," Tess said, watching the inept operation. "He was incredibly nervous. Made me nervous on his behalf."

"It'll be a good show on Thursday. I need a new biscuit. Want one?" Tess shook her head. Eric headed for the kitchenette where the urn and biscuits were.

Tess cupped her mug in her hands. It would be a good show. David would be brilliant. He couldn't help it. As soon as that violin was tucked under his chin and he lifted his bow a change came over him. She could almost see the calm and the concentrated focus cleansing the nervousness from his system. His stance altered, his face took on a dreamlike expression. Nothing registered beyond the music and his instrument. He was absorbed into the sounds surrounding him. She remembered it from years ago at the music school. Making music was the most important thing in his life.

Was there room for anything else? Any *one* else? Tess took a small gulp of tea. Had he any idea how much she wanted him to like her? Not just like her but respect her. It seemed that he did but the passion she'd always harbored for him had begun to crystallize during the week. The student fantasy of having David Montgomery in her life had become the reality of having David Montgomery in her house. Now that reality had opened up the possibility of things more intimate, unlikely as that may seem at the moment. David Montgomery was aware of her as a person for the first time. From person to woman was but a short step and from woman to girlfriend was even shorter in her experience. If she had his undivided attention she could make that happen. He couldn't completely hide that male attraction to her despite his reserve.

First, though, he had to sign on for a month in the house. Just for starters. His first week was almost up.

A few moments later David broke from the crowd and headed for her corner. He gave an exaggerated sigh of relief and smiled as he approached.

"Went well," she said. "You sounded marvelous."

"Do you really think so?" His eyes bored into hers anxious to believe the words were sincere and not just meaningless flattery.

"Yes. The last movement in particular—good, jaunty pace. I think some people play it too fast."

"I'm relying on you to tell me the truth," he said sternly.

Tess laughed. "Would I lie to you?"

"I hope not."

"About music? Never."

David's eyebrows rose quizzically but he didn't follow that up. Instead he said, "Can I ride home with you after the rehearsal? I'll stay to hear the Mahler."

Stuart arrived at lunchtime on Wednesday. Fid scampered down the hall with ears pricked ready to greet the intruder as the front door opened after a cursory knock. David, in the kitchen making an omelet for lunch, paused, listening. Tess splashed water about in the laundry in an attempt at hand washing a blouse.

"Hello, Fid. How are you?" The voice rang out strongly, the tread sounded purposeful in the hallway. "Anyone home? Tess? You there?" The front door clicked shut.

David wiped his hands carefully and prepared to meet the brother Tess was so in awe of. A compact, sandy-haired man in a very well-made charcoal gray suit appeared. He smiled when he spied David and held out the hand unencumbered with an overnight suit bag and briefcase. Very similar to Tess, strikingly so, the smile and the blue eyes. "Stuart Fuller," he said. "David? Very nice to meet you." Confident, very much the executive.

"Likewise." David shook the proffered hand firmly. "Tess is in the laundry. I'll fetch her."

"No, don't bother. I'll dump my gear. Where's she put me? Lavender Room?"

"I'm in there, sorry. I'm not sure where . . ."

"No worries." Stuart turned and headed back down the hall with Fid trotting after him. David continued whisking eggs. This was going to be interesting. Tess had anxiously told him at breakfast not to mention the Diva unless specifically asked and then he was to stick to her story of "the Mercedes belongs to a friend." She was mad and she was sure to be found out but that was all her problem—her brother, not his.

No way would he be concerning himself with her silliness with the performance tomorrow night.

So far so good with the City. This morning had been the dress rehearsal and sound check in the Concert Hall at the Opera House. Viktor had expressed his delight in no uncertain terms and he was notoriously hard to please. The violin section gushed with enthusiasm and the rest of the City had been nothing but warm and welcoming. All he needed now was a quiet evening and a relaxed day tomorrow. Perhaps a swim in the morning and some practice followed by a sleep after lunch.

David took his omelet and salad to the table. Tess had declined his offer to cook one for her saying a tub of yogurt would do. Stuart reappeared at the exact same moment Tess burst through from the laundry saying something about Hannibal.

"Stuey! When did you arrive?" She raced across and flung her arms around him.

Stuart returned the hug and kiss. "Five minutes ago. You're looking good."

"I am. Had lunch?"

"No, I'm meeting the Japanese team in about an hour at the Waterside Restaurant in Rose Bay."

"Did you meet David?"

"Yes." Stuart grinned past her at David. "I haven't got time to chat now, sorry. Tess, can I borrow your car?"

David glanced at Tess with his mouth full of lettuce and tomato. So quickly the subject had arisen. He chewed, watching her for signs of fluster or guilt. Not the slightest tremor crossed her face. "I'll drive you. I need the car later."

"Fine. If it's no trouble."

"No," she said. "Anyway I shouldn't let you drive it, it's not mine."

"What? The Toyota?"

"No, it's a Mercedes. A convertible."

"Where's the Toyota?" he demanded.

David stopped chewing and swallowed. Good point. Had she figured out an explanation for the lack of her old car?

"It's getting fixed." Of course she had. Tess was a consummate storyteller. A fibber.

"And someone loaned you their convertible Merc in the meantime?" Stuart's eyes opened wide in astonishment.

Tess frowned. "Why not? What's wrong with that?"

Stuart laughed. "Tessie, Tessie. A Merc? It must be worth a fortune. Who on earth would let *you* drive their Merc?"

"I'm a very good driver!" she cried. "Aren't I, David? He's been out with me, we go to rehearsals together."

Stuart looked at David with an incredulous expression. "You're a brave man."

"We arrive in one piece." For heaven's sake don't involve him. This was her fabrication.

"All I can say is the owner must be insane. Who is it?"

"No one you know," said Tess crossly. "He's away for a few weeks and I'm minding it. Do you want a lift or not?"

"Yes, please."

"I'll get my bag." She darted away toward her bedroom.

Stuart wandered across and sat on one of the stools by the bench. "I love her dearly," he said. "But she's a total nutcase."

"She's a very good musician." That offhand dismissal of Tess pricked uncomfortably. Had she had to endure that attitude all her life? From her brother *and* her father?

"Well, yes, but in any practical sense she's not much use." David ate more omelet to avoid responding to the blatant insult Stuart had no idea he'd just casually dropped. "Had much luck with the house hunting?"

"I've only looked at a few places so far. I wanted to get the performance out of the way first."

"The property market is very tight at the moment. Rents are sky-high. My rental property interests are making a killing." Stuart spoke with great satisfaction. "Here and in Melbourne. Which area are you looking in?"

"Inner north shore or city. Close to the rehearsal hall makes sense but I'd like somewhere close to a beach."

Stuart nodded.

David went on, "I was lucky Tess had the room free. I'd love to stay on here but neither of us wants to share. It's tempting though, especially now I've seen what's on offer."

Stuart frowned. He was about to speak but Tess charged in saying, "Come on. It'll take forty minutes to get across the harbor."

"See you later, David."

"Bye."

When Tess returned David was practicing. She went to the study to do her own work and an hour later he tapped on the door.

"Cup of tea?"

"Love one, thanks." She put her viola in its case and joined him in the kitchen, which had that unmistakable afterpong.

"The Phantom's been here," he said. "My eyes are watering."

Tess ran giggling to fling the French doors open.

David placed two mugs of tea on the bench. "Do you play any chamber music?" he asked as she perched herself on a stool.

"Not lately. We formed a string quartet a while back but with Oscar retiring up North it fizzled."

"Would you consider reviving it?"

"With you?"

"Yes."

"I'll talk to the others. We had Oscar and Eleanor, she leads the seconds, me and George, lead cellist."

"He's a superb player."

"And a lovely bloke." Tess downed some tea. Time to broach the delicate subject of next week's rent. Have to get it all sorted without Stuart hovering around. His timing couldn't have been worse, coming this week of all weeks. At least he'd accepted the car story without too much flak. She'd expected the slinging off at her driving ability but he'd been very impressed by the car itself. "Have you decided what you're going to do about a place to live?"

"No," he admitted. "Beyond hating those dumps we looked at I kind of put it out of my mind."

"Well, your funded week will be up on Friday."

He nodded. "And you want a commitment or a vacant room."

"Yep."

David studied her face for a moment. His eyes narrowed slightly as if trying to read her mind.

"What?"

"Why do I get the feeling you're not telling me something?"

"I have no idea," Tess replied with great dignity accompanied by the Fuller look, perfected by her father for use on anyone who questioned his judgment in any way. Direct and poker faced, no hint of a smile, slightly raised chin. Ice-cold. Unfortunately it didn't work on David.

"That almost proves it." He chuckled. "Okay. How about I give you one month in advance—twelve hundred dollars? That will give me time to look properly and you won't get your knickers in a twist about the Diva for a while."

Tess shot out her hand. "Done! In cash."

His fingers closed over hers. "Done. Drive me to the bank and we're in business."

"Fine. Hey! Your car-minding story was a great idea; Stu didn't even question it."

"I'd hardly say that and I really don't want to be implicated in your subterfuges, thanks."

"Too late, you already are," Tess called as she skipped down the hall to her room for bag and keys. "You're my accomplice," she yelled.

David woke early. He lay for a moment listening to a bird chirruping outside. Then, unable to stay immobile with his brain working overtime on Beethoven, jumped out of bed. A swim. Perfect. The best way to release that pent-up nervous tension. A jog down to Balmoral Beach, a brisk swim and perhaps a jog along the sand, then home for breakfast.

To his surprise Stuart was already up, drinking water in the kitchen in shorts and with a towel draped over his arm.

"Going for a swim?" David nodded. "Me too. Always do when I stay here." He put his empty juice glass in the dishwasher. "Ready?"

"I was going to run," said David.

"Fine. Let's go."

The sun had only just cleared the horizon and he blinked against the rays slanting directly into his eyes as they turned at the bottom of the drive and headed downhill. Stuart paced easily beside him, obviously a seasoned runner. He swung left at the corner where Tess and David had walked right. "Better route this way," he said.

David breathed deeply. He could feel the tension literally melting away with the rhythmic pounding of feet on tar and the fresh salt air cleansing his lungs. Stuart was a good companion. He didn't insist on talking, unlike his sister who couldn't stop. A smile creased his lips unexpectedly at the thought of Tess. What a crazy girl. What on earth was she up to? The next month would be interesting. Had he made the biggest blunder of his life by handing over a month's rent in advance? He'd never prise it out of her if she changed her mind for some reason or if they had a massive falling out. No. He was ensconced in that house for a month come hell or high water.

"That Merc is some car," said Stuart after a time. "Whose is it, do you know?"

"She already had it when I arrived." Not really a lie, not really an answer.

The beach appeared. Stuart's route had led them around to the far end from where he and Tess had swum. They paused to allow a car to pass then pounded across the road to the grass, plowed through soft white sand and steadied to an even pace again on the hard strip near the water.

Stuart grunted. "I hope she doesn't damage it before the owner reclaims it."

"She's a pretty good driver."

They negotiated the little bridge to the island and ran to the rocks at the end of the small beach. Half way back Stuart stopped. "Swim?"

"Sure."

Tess rolled over, sat up, yawned, and stretched her arms out front then over her head. Sunlight streamed in when she yanked open the curtains. Lovely morning. Shower first then some tai chi—that new move they'd learned last lesson was very complicated, needed heaps of practice. David should come with her to classes if he was seriously interested. He wouldn't learn anything useful from her inept version.

The house was silent when she emerged. Stu was probably running or down at the beach. He always swam when he stayed here. David too? Heavens! Please let him be sleeping. Tess raced to the Lavender Room. The bathroom was empty, the bedroom door ajar. She tiptoed closer and carefully pushed it wider, peeped in. Empty. They were out together. Disaster! They'd be talking and the only thing they had in common was her. And David didn't know not to discuss the rental situation.

Breathing hard and fast Tess blindly retraced her steps to the kitchen. She stopped in the middle of the floor, eyes closed, fists clenched, chest heaving. But maybe he hadn't said anything. Why would he? The thought popped her eyes open. David didn't talk for talking's sake. Stu preferred to talk about business. Maybe, just maybe, she was safe. But she'd have to prime David, feed him a little bit of the truth—enough to make sure he didn't say he'd given her a month's rent. Why did Stu have to turn up right now? And why did Daddy have to make such a stupid will?

Voices. The front door opened and closed. Footsteps thudded in the hall. Tess plastered a smile on her face and grabbed the jug to fill it under the tap.

"Good morning. You making coffee, Tess?" asked Stu.

"Tea, actually, but I can do coffee." David wiped his face with his towel as he passed. Threw her a smile.

Stu grinned. "Great. And fruit if you have any."

"Of course I do," she called after him. He was already headed for the bathroom. No worries! They hadn't had a heart to heart, obviously. She switched the kettle on and hurried after David. He turned, surprised, in the doorway. She shoved him through gently and closed the door to the family area behind them. "I have something to tell you."

He tilted his head to one side, eyebrows raised, expression bland. "Hurry up. I want a shower."

"It's about Stu. Did you—" She faltered.

"I didn't spill the beans on the Diva," he interrupted swiftly. "That all?" He stepped into the bathroom and stripped off his sweat-stained T-shirt. Tess stifled a gasp at the sudden, unexpected sight of tanned bare torso glistening with perspiration. He dropped the garment on the floor and faced her. Hot male swamped her nostrils, all her senses. "Are you going to stay and watch?" he asked with a tiny smile.

"Oooh, can I?" And scrub his back for him? Her face must have revealed her lascivious thoughts because he laughed, shaking his head. "Tess, Tess, Tess." He looked up and around then down into her face. "No. Have you finished?"

"Not exactly." Those eyes of his were simply gorgeous, all soft and tender with laughter. He really did like her. How much?

"Well?"

"Stu would be angry if he knew I was renting to you," she said delicately.

"You already said that."

"Did I?"

He nodded. "The first morning. You said he didn't like the idea of strangers in the house."

"Oh. No, he doesn't."

"But I'm not a stranger, am I? He knows me now." He touched her cheek with a light finger and smiled. "Is that what you're worried about? He won't approve of me?"

Tess licked her lips. "Sort of." Her brain had gone into meltdown. His finger slid to her chin. Then away. She sighed at the loss.

But his tone hardened. "Sort of?" No tenderness at all.

"I'm not really—allowed to have tenants." The last words tumbled out. She held her breath.

"Allowed?" he demanded. "Says who? What are you talking about?" His eyes were dark muddy pools of anger now. And suspicion. Tess released the pent-up air and collapsed onto the edge of the bath. He glared at her, hands on hips, deep furrows in his brow. "What have you got me into, Tess? No lies."

She glared up at him defiantly. Why did he assume she'd lie? "It's Daddy's will. It's really unfair—he left the house to me under the condition I live here and don't marry or rent it or have anyone else renting with me until I'm thirty-five. I have to have Stuart's permission up till then to do just about anything short of breathing."

"Why on earth would your father do that?" David's voice rose incredulously.

Tess couldn't meet his gaze. She stared at her bare feet instead. No option but the truth, he wouldn't accept less. He'd know. "He didn't trust me not to do something stupid."

"And what's the penalty if you break the terms of the will?" His voice was a hammer, hard and merciless.

"The house reverts to Stuart and I have to leave."

"So you've risked the house, your home, for that car and implicated me in this law breaking."

Tess leaped to her feet. "It's not law breaking. It's a stupid will! Daddy was convinced I wasn't capable of looking after this place properly. He was a chauvinistic tyrant; he never believed I could do anything. He didn't like my friends and he didn't like my—" Her mouth clamped shut seconds too late, five words too late.

"Your what?" Deadly cold now.

No point lying, he may as well know the lot. And so what? He already thought she was a disaster area. "My husband," she whispered.

"You're married?" He stepped back against the shower wall with such a horrified, stunned expression her heart shriveled. But all the old defense mechanisms sprang to her aid. The ones that had supported her through that first stupidity and more recently the Raoul blunder.

She gave him the Fuller look. "No. It only lasted two weeks. One summer. I was eighteen. It was over before it began."

"My heavens! No wonder he didn't trust you! I'm amazed he left you anything at all!" He looked at her as though she was something repulsive, something despicable to be avoided at all costs. "Although I don't suppose he expected to die so soon, so young. Before you turned thirty-five and were presumably more mature. How old are you?"

"Thirty-two."

"He should have made it fifty."

Tess glared at him. "I don't see why you're so upset about it. I'm the one who loses if Stuart finds out, not you."

"Oh, I just lose twelve hundred dollars. I guess that's peanuts to you." Such contempt on his face she couldn't bear it. "You haven't changed a bit, Tess. You're still that mindless, irresponsible eighteen-year-old."

"What are you going to do?" she said, fearful he'd suddenly take his outrage and his self-righteous honesty straight to Stuart. He turned away from her to lean on the hand basin, head bowed. "He needn't know anything about our deal," she said in exasperation. He shook his head, still lowered.

"I've never done a dishonest thing in my life," he muttered.

"This isn't dishonest."

"You just can't see it, can you?" He turned slowly. "Little Spoiled Rich Girl, can't even control herself long enough to . . ." He flung his hands apart. "What's the use?"

"Will you tell him?"

"I should . . ."

Tess gasped at the sheer, unnecessary, troublemaking spite of the man. He ignored her outraged expression.

"But I won't. Just give me my money back and I'll move out. I don't want anything to do with you or your lies, Tess."

She exhaled slowly, sagged with relief then his words sank in. Give his money back? "But . . ."

"That's all." He stared at her waiting for her to leave.

"I can't give you your money back. I put it straight into the loan and I don't have enough spare cash at the moment."

His mouth opened. His eyes closed momentarily. "Of course," he murmured.

"I can pay you back in installments."

"And how am I supposed to come up with bond money and rent in the meantime? Moving house is expensive, Tess. *I* need to buy a car too and I don't want to be funding *your* extravagance instead. Although you wouldn't know anything about managing finances, would you?"

Tess swallowed. He only had one option. "You'll have to stay."

He raised his hand as he stepped forward and she took a step back instinctively. But he grabbed the bathroom door instead and shut it in her face.

Chapter Six

David spun the hot tap with a vicious twist of the wrist. He waited till steam rose wisping into the air then adjusted the cold inflow. How could she do that? He'd asked her several times to her face what she was up to and she'd looked right back with those big blue eyes and said, "Nothing." Like a total idiot he'd believed her. A total idiot who'd *wanted* to believe her, believe she thought he was different from all those other men she'd fooled. Had a special claim because he'd known her before. He wasn't different; he was exactly the same. He was just as smitten by her looks and bubbly personality as the rest. Thank goodness he hadn't succumbed to the invitation clear in her eyes.

He stripped off his shorts and swimmers and stepped under the cascade. What was he supposed to do now?

He couldn't stay here after Friday. What a hideously awful mess. On the most important day of his life so far too. Had she thought of that when she blithely told him her little problem? No, she'd been thinking of number one, as usual. Not even the slightest consideration of his mental state on performance day. How could he possibly concentrate tonight? How could he relax this afternoon?

She'd better keep well out of his way! He thought they were friends. How could she lie like that? Use him, manipulate him? Is that what she'd done to that poor sod Raoul?

By the time he'd showered, dressed, and calmed down enough to go to the kitchen for breakfast, Stuart had left and Tess was practicing in the study. He made tea. The viola stopped. He froze with his hand on the toaster, gritted his teeth against her appearance. Rich sounds started up again. Part of his mind registered she was playing Mahler and very well, the troublesome phrases smoothed during the week flowing freely now, on concert day. The other, betrayed part still cried, "How could you?"

He pressed the lever and his bread disappeared. Dirty breakfast plates and cutlery lay untidily on the bench and in the sink. Stuart must be as messy as his sister. He folded his arms and waited for the toaster. His jaw ached. His teeth were clamped together and he consciously relaxed his bite. When the toast popped he buttered and spread marmalade and took the plate and his mug of tea outside. Fid lay snoozing on the warm pavement. He raised his head and flopped his tail but didn't get up.

David forced himself to eat despite his appetite having shrunk to nothing. He always felt this way before a performance. He always forced down food and felt better. But this was far worse than usual with the overlay of shock and disappointment, the betrayal of trust by a woman he'd begun to . . . No! The viola sang on. He had to put her out of his mind, had to concentrate for this evening, continue with his day as planned. She was a beautiful player. Did Stuart realize how talented she was? Didn't sound like it. He was the sort of guy who calculated value in dollar terms. Wasn't above impressing his business associates by taking them to a concert though and would undoubtedly want to bring them backstage afterward to meet the soloist and conductor.

What a family. And he thought he'd had it tough growing up with brothers who had cloth ears and parents with little money. At least in his crazy mob they'd all known they were loved and they all supported each other with great pride regardless of occupation. From those humble beginnings had sprung a wildlife ranger, another mechanic like Dad, a gardener and himself. He went inside for the phone and more tea, and sat for half an hour in the garden chatting to unshakable, dependable Mum about the goings-on in Cootamundra.

At five, Tess tapped tentatively on David's door. He opened it and glared down at her.

"I'm sorry to disturb you," she said. "But would you like to drive in with me tonight?"

It had been a given before. Now she wasn't so sure. His face was shadowed and tense. So nervous, his stomach would be knotted. She wanted to hug him and reassure him, help him relax, take his mind off the concert. He hated her, and she felt sick.

"I don't need to be there as early as you," he said. "I've ordered a taxi."

"All right." The door began closing. "David? Have you decided what you're going to do?"

"About staying here?"

She nodded. "And about the other thing—telling Stuart."

"No. I have other things on my mind at the moment."

The door closed firmly. Tess stood irresolute, twisting her hands together. How could she tell him what she really wanted? To wish him luck, that he'd play brilliantly. She was sorry . . .

She lifted her hand to tap but lost her nerve and fled to the study where she double-checked her concert music and viola. Fid and Hannibal needed dinner so she attended to that and came back inside to prepare her own light meal—tofu and stir-fry vegetables. Must force something down although the way her stomach felt it might throw everything straight back up.

What about David? He'd want to eat something. He'd have to or he'd have no energy for Beethoven. Performing solo was an incredibly exhausting experience, physically and emotionally. More so this time—such an important milestone for him. Had she completely spoiled it? Surely not. He was a seasoned professional. In fact, he may even play better after an emotional shake-up. Or not. Tess drew a deep breath for courage and strode to the passageway door. It opened before she had a chance to touch the handle.

He stared at her briefly then edged past. She ignored the icy demeanor and leaped right in. "I was just coming to ask if you wanted something to eat." She followed his stiff-backed march to the kitchen, trailing after him the way Fid trailed after her.

He surveyed the half-peeled carrot and the small pile of assorted vegetables waiting to go into the wok. "What is it?"

"Vegetable and tofu stir-fry."

"Yes, I'll have some, thanks."

Tess grabbed the peeler and continued where she'd left off—another carrot and more beans and snowpeas. David poured himself a glass of water and wandered across to the table. He sat down in front of the paper with the crossword.

"Is Stuart coming home for dinner?" he asked.

"No. He's eating in town with his business friends. They'll go straight to the concert."

He drained the glass. "I'll stay the month. But only because I have no choice. Don't think I've forgiven you, Tess, or that I condone what you're doing in any way, shape, or form."

Tess kept her head lowered over her chopping board. Thank goodness, thank goodness, thank goodness. She lit the gas under the wok and poured in a dash of oil trying desperately not to let him see the smile waiting to burst forth.

He said with a certain amount of spite. "You realize the whole orchestra knows you're searching for a tenant and that Stuart knows them."

"No, he doesn't. Only Ian, and Ian won't talk about my private affairs with him. They'll talk about sponsorship money and business." In went the onion.

David grunted skeptically.

Tess added, "Stuart won't talk to the musicians when there are more important people around—board members, for example. And there are far more important topics of conversation than me." And thank heavens for that.

Garlic sizzled in with the onion pieces. Tess scraped and flipped. In went the other vegetables and the tofu with a good dollop of hoisin sauce. Three minutes later she spooned the steaming stir-fry into two bowls and ferried them with forks and soy sauce to the table.

"Thanks." He poked at a piece of broccoli.

"Eat," she said.

"I never feel hungry before a concert."

"Neither do I but I always eat something." Tess speared tofu as he chewed slowly. "You'll be fine."

"I wanted a quiet, relaxing day." His gaze remained

on his food. "First I had you, then this afternoon that wretched vacuum cleaner."

"Sorry. I forgot Rita was coming. I stopped her from doing your room, though."

"You could economize by doing the cleaning yourself." The look he gave her was poisonous.

Tess gritted her teeth. "The house is too big. And Stuart insists it's done properly."

David pushed his bowl away and stood up. "Thanks for dinner." He left the dish on the table and went to his room. She heard water running and a toothbrush scrubbing.

A month of this? How could things have gone from right to wrong so quickly? A friendship had been established the preceding week, one that had survived the arrows from the bass section and the sniping of Yvonne. He didn't hold her affair with Raoul against her, had seemed to accept her past aberrations as irrelevant to the present, and even though she had a lot of ground to make up as far as resetting his basic, albeit inaccurate, party girl opinion of her, she'd seemed to be making headway.

Until Stuart messed things up. If only his Japanese contacts had chosen another time or another city to meet. Tess stacked the bowls and cutlery to take to the kitchen. She scraped the leftovers into the bin. A sigh escaped as she straightened. David had made a valid point, one that she'd only vaguely considered. Realistically she couldn't hide a tenant from Stuart for very long. He'd think it was odd that every time he came to Sydney she had someone visiting—the same someone. David for the next month wouldn't be a problem, Stu had accepted his presence without any suspicions at all and knew he was searching for his own place. But in the long term?

A stodgy lump settled in her belly. Without that rent money she'd be stretched very tight financially. The upkeep on the house was huge—insurance, rates, local council taxes, repairs, cleaning, gardening, and that was before her own expenses. Plus the Diva's. And not forgetting Hannibal's spiraling medical bills. All her planning had relied on an external income to fund the loan. Was the Diva doomed?

Dressed in long, black concert gear Tess tapped on David's door. "I'm leaving soon," she called. "Are you sure you don't want a lift?"

The door remained closed. She tapped louder. "David?" No reply. Not there. Perhaps he'd gone out for a walk to calm down. Should she peek in to make quite sure he hadn't dropped dead on the floor? After the bawling out she'd received last time, better not. Perhaps he was out in the studio warming up. That would be it. Better not disturb him, she'd done enough disrupting today and he was very fragile at the moment. A quick check confirmed Fid's lead was missing.

Tess gathered her things together and headed for the

garage. David wouldn't want to come in yet anyway because he'd have to sit around for at least an hour. The orchestra had to be there a minimum half an hour before concert time and Tess preferred that to be forty minutes. The first item on the program took fifteen minutes so the Beethoven wouldn't be on until at least 8:20. It was now 6:45. He'd probably aim to arrive about 7:45. Yes, no need for him to leave now. Still . . . she did want to wish him luck. Leaving without seeing him felt wrong. He probably thought it felt right. If he spared her a thought at all.

The Diva burst into life. Tess backed down the drive and turned for the Opera House. Smooth and luxurious Diva. She couldn't possibly give up this fabulous car.

David returned from his walk calmer but still in a familiar state of nervous tension. The taxi was booked for 7:15. Twenty-five minutes to dress. Perfect. Tess had gone. She hadn't wished him luck. But it was probably good not to have seen her. The last thing he needed was to be reminded of her behavior and that whole horrible thing this morning. She hadn't even waited to say good-bye. He'd see her at the Concert Hall. Perhaps he should have gone in with her. She hadn't given him a chance to change his mind, leaving that way before he returned home.

Focus. Beethoven.

The taxi was late. David phoned at 7:20, more knots

forming on the knots already in his stomach. A phone queue. He slammed the phone down and immediately snatched it up again to dial Ian's mobile.

"I'll send someone," Ian said calmly. "Why didn't you come with Tess?"

"She left too early."

"All right. Sit tight."

David sat in the living room with the curtains open so as to see a car, or better still the taxi, when it arrived. He checked his watch for the fiftieth time. Half past seven now. Impossible to sit still any longer. He collected his violin and went to wait on the road in the pool of light from the streetlight. Lovely evening, if he'd had the time or inclination to enjoy the balmy breeze and the warm stillness of the darkened street. Leaves rustled gently overhead. A strong perfume wafted into his nostrils, then was gone. A car swished by. Quiet. In the distance a siren howled. Stopped. Another car. His eyes strained hopefully. Taxi? No. It turned in two doors along.

His ride must be here soon. How long would it take? Depended on traffic—twenty minutes? What if whoever they sent got lost? Thirty? Forty-five minutes round-trip? He'd still be there in time. They couldn't start the Beethoven without him.

Five minutes later an unmistakable engine roared as a car rounded the corner and accelerated toward him. Dazzling headlights cut across his face. Blinking. Spots before his eyes. The Diva swung into the driveway. He grabbed his violin and flung the door open.

Tess grinned from the driver's seat. "Hi there, sailor. Wanna go for a ride?"

She was reversing even as he closed the door. He found the seat belt and fastened it firmly, violin wedged between his knees. No doubt he'd be needing that seat belt. At least she'd put the top up tonight.

"What are you doing here? Shouldn't you be playing Rossini?" It sounded grudging and surly when really he was overwhelmed she would come herself. Tess, unpredictable as ever. He glanced across. Her eyes were focused intently on the road. She'd done something to her hair with a clasp so the delicate shell of her ear was exposed and a sparkle of silvery diamonds swung when she moved her head. Real ones, of course. The line of her jaw, softly curved and vulnerable, tempted his fingers before he remembered her perfidy.

The Diva accelerated briefly then slowed at the Give Way at the end of their road, paused momentarily for a car, charged across and turned right.

She said, "We might make it in time but Ian said it won't matter if I don't. The violas'll move up a desk. You're the important thing."

"Heavens, Tess." He clung on grimly as they shot out onto Military Road, narrowly missing a motorbike and a bus. "Thank you. I think."

"I made it here in seventeen minutes," she announced. "I told Ian I'd be fastest because I know where to go."

"And you drive like a maniac." And she loved every hair-raising minute, he'd bet his last cent.

Tess laughed. "Aren't you glad?"

Sheer relief and an overload of adrenaline forced a laugh. "I must admit—yes. I am." Very, very glad. Tess, with her smile and her infectious, exhilarating bravado in the face of this near disaster. Forgiving. Far more so than he.

"You'll give the best performance of your life." She spoke with such absolute confidence he believed her despite the fact she was lane changing with unnerving speed on the freeway approach to the massive arch of the Harbour Bridge. "See, we're nearly there."

The Opera House gleamed pearly white in its flood-lights, jutting out into the harbor, commanding attention. Such a familiar Sydney landmark, known throughout the world, an Australian icon. And he was about to perform on the stage in the Concert Hall with the City Symphony Orchestra. Unbelievable.

The Diva sailed across the bridge and plunged into the muddle of exit lanes. Tess knew exactly where she was going with the unerring focus and speed of a heat-seeking missile. Then a frustrating stop-start through the lights near Circular Quay and a marginally more sedate swing into the forecourt of the Opera House. He glanced at the clock on the dash—six minutes past eight. Then they were in the underground car park cruising for a space. Found one. Out of the Diva. Whoop of the alarm. Hurrying, violin in hand, between rows of parked cars to the exit stairs. Tess striding beside him with a grin from ear to ear, face flushed and lovely with excitement and a touch of pride. Black suited her, the raised hairstyle showed off her neck, made her look sophisticated, a refined woman rather than a crazy girl. Her dress clung to her figure with restrained elegance. Classy style from head to toe.

He stopped, grabbed her bare arm, warm under his fingers. She looked up into his face, those blue eyes wide with surprise and a hint of alarm.

"Thanks," he said before she could speak, and bent quickly to kiss her. Aimed for her cheek but found soft lips instead. Paused in amazement, delight, a shocking punch of desire. Nothing registered except lips on lips. Such sweetness, such . . . pleasure. So right, so perfect. Her mouth moved gently against his—just for an instant, an endless, world-shattering instant.

She sighed, drew away. She was speaking. He heard her through a rush of emotion. Dimly.

"We'd better go," she murmured.

Why? Beethoven. "Yes."

She hurried him to the stage entrance beneath the vast expanse of steps that rose to the upper levels of the Opera House. No time to wonder, no time to consider. Security. Signatures, passes. Negotiated. She led; he followed. She wouldn't look at him. Couldn't? Was she offended, angry, upset? No, not Tess. Party Girl. Once married. Worse, was she laughing at such a pathetic, boyish attempt at a kiss? While he . . . They ran through the corridor to the large central Green Room. Opening bars of Beethoven springing into his head. Strong decisive chords. Soon. Headed into another maze of passageways to the backstage area. Faint strains of Rossini sounding through the PA system. Just started. Not late at all. Wonderful Tess.

Ian hovered expectantly. Smiled with relief when they appeared. "This way, David." He ushered him to a dressing room. Tess hung back, disappeared somewhere. "Tess made good time. We started five minutes late so you've got about twenty minutes to catch your breath."

David placed his violin on the bench beneath a row of mirrors lit for makeup application. Time slowed, lurched to the present. His performance was imminent. The first appearance in this new role. His audience waited, wondering at his ability. Such a stupid and undignified beginning. He turned to Ian. "I'm sorry this happened. Tess should have been playing, not being a taxi driver."

Ian slapped him on the back. "No worries. She jumped at the chance to drive that car. She's like a kid with a new toy."

"She is." He opened the case and lifted his old familiar, his best friend, his violin. Together they'd conquer anything.

"I'll leave you to warm up. There'll be a five-minute call."

"I'll come and listen before then."

"Fine." Ian gave him a thumbs-up and backed out.

David commenced his warm-up exercises. Muscles relaxed, breathing slowed, the trance began.

Tess dumped her bag next to her viola case and sat down heavily on the nearest chair. He kissed her. A thank-you kiss? Must have been. He was panicky and flying on adrenaline, worried about not getting to the hall on time. Relief made him do it. He probably would have kissed Ian if he'd been driving. Meant nothing—to him.

Ian poked his head round the partially open door. "Thanks, Tess."

"No problem." What a kiss. Too short. So sweet, so tender. Would there be any more? Ever?

"Rossini's about half over," Ian said.

She concentrated on his disembodied face, computing what he'd just said. "Oh—fine." She grinned. "I must have set a world record. About forty minutes round-trip."

"Not a record I'd be trying to break." He raised his eyebrows, gave a short bark of laughter, and disappeared.

Tess waited in the wings for *The Thieving Magpie* to swoop to its finish. David stood beside her, apparently calm. She snuck a little peek. He seemed relaxed, no nervous clenching of the jaw, just listening intently, not thinking of anything other than the music. Certainly not thinking about her. Or that kiss. Why would he? Sudden applause brought her sharply into focus. The orchestra rose to take their bow. Viktor strode offstage, beaming when he saw David beside her. He'd have had no idea if they'd arrived safely. Poor Viktor.

He grasped David's hand. "Ready?"

"Yes."

The players not needed in the concerto came offstage. Tess moved quickly into her place beside Matt, who shifted across to his usual chair while Jane went back a desk and the rest shuffled into place. Back to normal. David hadn't even glanced at her. Too focused. In the zone.

"Did you find him?" whispered Matt.

Tess nodded. Her stomach was churning now. Not for her own performance but for David's. He hadn't had an ideal preparation today. His routine had been completely disrupted, the all-important mental focus scattered every which way. But he was a wonderful player, a professional. He'd cope. But would he play as well as he wanted? He'd fool the audience easily enough because he couldn't play badly if he tried but his harshest critic would be himself. He'd been aiming for this moment all his life as a violinist. This was a personal goal, an achievement some would regard as a stepping stone to other, greater things but which for him would give the greatest satisfaction. She couldn't bear to be the cause of a less-than-brilliant performance.

She raised her viola to her shoulder and tuned carefully. Viktor marched onstage to take his place on the podium. The applause strengthened as he raised his arm to welcome David, the soloist.

Striding out before his audience David focused on Viktor, mouth dry, fingers clammy. A glimpse of pale faces in the front rows staring, hands flailing. The clapping increased, thundering around the capacity hall as he bowed, then dying away abruptly when Viktor turned to face the orchestra, baton ready.

David caught Stan's eye and returned his smile. Silence. All eyes on Viktor. The first notes emerged from the strings and wind. David closed his eyes. The main theme climbed, the orchestra gathered strength, immersing him. He fingered the familiar neck of his fiddle, lifted the instrument to his chin, and played a few bars with the first violins, checking the intonation, releasing the pressure of nerves stretched taut. Relaxed. Beethoven took hold. Viktor drove the introduction along strongly. Good tempo. Excellent orchestra. Must do them and himself justice.

His entry neared. Five bars, three, two. In. Strong decisive chords, ascending, striving, soaring . . .

Then it was over. Crashing applause. Viktor beaming and pumping his hand, clapping him on the back. Bowing. Shaking Stan's hand, acknowledging the orchestra. More bows. Offstage. Pushed back on by Viktor. Tess smiling and clapping with the rest of the musicians, some tapping their bows on the music stands. Impossible to catch her eye. A young woman thrust a gift-wrapped bottle of wine into his hand. Applause going on and on. Offstage again. On again. Off. The applause faded at last, replaced by a roar of voices. House lights up. Interval.

David stood with Ian and Viktor drinking in their approval. His dress shirt under the black jacket was soaked with perspiration. He didn't care. Adrenaline still pumped through his body. Exhilarating. He'd played well, very well. Smiles everywhere. The players congratulated him as they filed offstage. Viktor was delighted.

"A magnificent performance," he said. "The slow movement was exquisite."

Ian said, "Remember, there's a small reception upstairs later, David. The sponsors and various others. You'll come?"

"Certainly. Yes, thank you."

Where was Tess? Had she gone offstage to the other side? People kept congratulating him. He smiled and acknowledged the praise, searching over their shoulders for the multitoned hair, the sparkling diamonds, the beaming smile. Not there.

He headed for the dressing room to pack away his violin. Down a glass of water. Surely she'd come to say . . . something. He closed the door on the hubbub of players. What an incredible thrill, an amazing high. He grinned at the man in the mirror. "You did it!" He laughed with delight.

The violin safely in its case, David removed his jacket and undid his bowtie. He sank into a chair with a glass of water. Someone knocked. Tess? Ian.

"I brought you a cup of coffee."

David put the glass down and took the proffered mug. "Thanks."

Ian sat down comfortably with his own coffee, leaning back in the chair. "We've quite a schedule coming up. I need to go over a few details with you."

"Now?" What timing. How to take the gloss off a performance in one easy lesson.

"No, no. Tomorrow will do. There's no rehearsal so come in about eleven. How are you getting on with Tess?'

An abrupt switch of topic. David glanced up sharply. "All right. Why do you ask?" Ian was far more perceptive than he'd initially given him credit for. Made a good manager.

"She seemed . . . not her usual self tonight when she arrived."

David took a thoughtful sip of coffee. Too much sugar for his taste but the gesture was nice. "Her brother is staying."

"Stuart. Do they not get on?"

"They seem to be genuinely attached to each other. Stuart and I went for a run and a swim together this morning. He doesn't seem to have a very high opinion of her ability, her profession. Our profession," he added with a lift of the eyebrows.

"His company sponsors the City. Of course they get a considerable tax benefit by doing so," Ian said dryly.

"He's brought his Japanese business colleagues along tonight."

"Yes. It's a classy night out. Doesn't do the corporate image any harm to take clients to the Opera House for a concert."

David nodded with a wry twist of a smile. What was a musician's lifeblood was just another commodity in corporate land. He said, "You know, I've fulfilled a childhood ambition tonight."

Ian tilted his head. "To play in the Opera House?"

"To play the Beethoven in the Opera House as concert master of the City Symphony."

"How very satisfying. What's next?"

David's smile faded. "To do the very best I can in my new job."

"No further ambitions as a soloist?"

Serious now. "Perhaps, yes. But I like the orchestral work. I love the repertoire."

"And what about personally? A family and so on?"

David shuddered theatrically. "Heavens no. I don't want anyone else to worry about. I want to focus on my music and I don't need any distractions, thank you. In my experience women are too much trouble and far too complicated. Children—I can't imagine."

Ian smiled with the indulgence of an elder who knows better but is too polite to say so. "Marriage isn't a distraction. My wife, Glenys, is the best thing that ever happened to me, and my children come a close second."

"Good for you." Someone knocked. Tess? "Come in," he called. The door opened on two smiling members of the board of directors and their wives.

Ian stood up. "I'd better get the troops moving. Well done, David. You made a magnificent debut with us."

"Here, here," said one of the newcomers. David rose and extended his hand. "Thank you very much."

Ian closed the door behind himself leaving David with his gushing fans.

After they'd left to regain their seats for the rest of the program, he drank the rest of the sweet, now cold coffee, and washed the taste down with a swig of water.

Ian's words played in his head. What was his next goal? He hadn't thought much beyond tonight. His new position, of course, would take priority. But marriage? Children? Good heavens. Nothing was further from his mind apart from the fact there was no likely female on the radar. Except Tess. He laughed. Marry Tess? That would be the ultimate in insanity.

Anyway she wouldn't be in the marriage stakes until she turned thirty-five or she'd lose that house. And Tess wouldn't be giving up any of her luxuries in a hurry. She was way too comfortable and far from denying herself, she'd learned ways to have her cake and eat it too. The Diva being a case in point. At his expense!

No, any man who took on Tess would be in for the roller coaster ride of his life and it would serve the idiot right.

The orchestra would go onstage for the Mahler in a few minutes. Why hadn't she come to see him?

Chapter Seven

Tess came offstage exhausted but exhilarated. Nothing else like it. The long symphony drained every emotion and was equally demanding on concentration and technique. They'd played well. Viktor was pleased and stood in the wings applauding them as they walked off.

"Thank goodness we've nothing till Monday," said Matt.

"Yes and the next program is easy."

"Coming for a drink?"

"Not tonight, thanks. I've had it." Some party girl she was. But she felt like chewed string. Physically and emotionally. Sleep would fix one but not the other.

Tess went straight to her case to pack away the viola. Where was David? Would he want a ride home? Probably not. He'd be off with the heavies celebrating somewhere.

Stu too, more than likely. They could go home together in a taxi.

She slipped on her jacket, picked up her bag and viola case and eased through the milling, chattering players looking for David. His dressing room was empty. She stood undecided, frowning. "Seen David Montgomery?" she asked a second violinist.

"Near the entrance with Ian."

Tess headed for the door. He was laughing, standing with Ian and an audience member, an attractive blond woman who gazed at him with total adoration. His teeth flashed white as he turned on the charm. Formal black suited him, the dignified outfit accentuated his physique, that well-maintained body. She knew firsthand just how well maintained. From the waist up, at least. And in swimmers. That blonde hadn't—but would love to judging by her expression. She was ready to eat him alive. Virtually slobbering in anticipation.

Tess marched up to the group. Blondie seared her with a pair of green eyes while her red-painted mouth smiled.

"Excuse me, please." Tess threw Ian and the groupie a smile. "David, I just wanted to check whether you'll be coming home with me now or if you've got other plans."

David looked down at her with a curious expression. "There's a reception. Stuart will be there—I thought—"

He glanced at Ian who promptly said, "Of course, come along, Tess. I'm sorry. I should've mentioned it earlier."

"Oh no. I don't think—" Dull, dull, dull. Board members whose average age was about ninety, Japanese businessmen, politicians, and sundry other bores. The only good thing would be free champagne except she wouldn't be able to drink any because she was driving. This was David's night and he wouldn't want her there, he'd made that pretty clear this morning. Keep out of his way. Work was one thing, socializing another.

The blonde simpered. "I'll make sure he gets home safely." Whose home? David didn't seem fazed by her blatant innuendo. Was she the sort of woman he liked? Vacuous? Why go along and watch him in action with her? Keep out of his way. That's what he wanted.

"Thanks, Ian, but I'm exhausted. Have fun, David. Good night."

She turned quickly and strode through the door and down the corridor, tense fingers jingling the Diva's keys in her pocket.

"Tess." His voice pulled her up sharply. He was annoyed. She turned around. Why should he be annoyed? He strode toward her, violin case and gift-wrapped bottle in hand. "Will you take these home for me, please?"

"Sure." Why not? She was the taxi driver.

He stopped a pace away. "Why won't you come?"

"I'm tired."

"No you're not."

"How do you know?"

"I know the high after a performance. You need to

unwind slowly." His eyes bored into hers. "You can't just go home and go to bed."

Tess dropped her gaze. He was right. She wouldn't sleep. For many reasons not least being him. A kiss. And the blonde. He stepped closer. "You didn't congratulate me. Didn't you think I played well?"

Tess grinned despite her turmoil and looked straight up into those dark, smiling eyes. "You played wonderfully well. You know you did. It was fantastic."

"Thank you. But you didn't come to tell me."

What was he on about? Did he really care? Plenty of people were telling him how well he played. "I didn't want to interrupt you. I saw Ian go in and shut the door."

"You could've joined us."

"Why is what I do so important to you all of a sudden?" Tess drew a deep breath. "I thought after what happened this morning I should keep away from you as much as possible."

"Mmm." His expression hardened. "What you did— you've done—" He spread his arms, shaking his head in disbelief. "Unbelievable."

"See? It's better if I go home. You go and enjoy yourself, you've earned it. Make Stu pay for the taxi home."

David sighed. "If you're positive. I thought you liked parties."

"I do but this one's not my type." The blonde tip-tapped down the corridor toward them. Tess caught her determined eye around David's shoulder. "Here comes your friend," she murmured.

"Who?" Eyes wide and startled. Pleasingly so. He'd truly forgotten the woman.

"I'll leave you to it." That blonde meant business. Well, Tess could play that game. Under the possessive green stare she stood on tiptoe, slipped one hand around his neck, and kissed him firmly on the lips. She remained transfixed for a long amazed instant because he responded. And it felt wonderful. Just like earlier. She recovered herself enough to draw away and say, "Good night," with cool control. Her eyes met his briefly. Puzzled. He looked puzzled and confused. But the blonde understood. She said crisply, "There you are! I thought I'd lost you. I'll take you up to the reception room, David."

He turned with a polite smile. Tess grabbed his violin, shoved the bottle under her arm, and walked away, head up, a pleased grin tugging at her mouth. Ha! Take that you blond bimbo. She'd get nowhere with a man like David. How disappointing for her.

But the confidence that she'd done the right thing by not attending the reception faded gradually as the night drew on and neither David nor Stuart returned home. Where were they? And were they together? Was the blond bimbo involved? The official gathering would be long over. They only lasted an hour at most. Half the guests needed adrenaline shots just to remain upright and awake after nine o'clock.

Tess twisted around in bed to stare at the luminous numbers on her bedside clock: 12:43. If the men had gone off somewhere together after the reception there was no cause to worry. If they hadn't—if Stu had taken his Japanese friends out to see Sydney's nightlife and left David with the BB—then she'd made a massive mistake. Stupid idiot, thinking she knew how his mind worked based on the young man of eleven years ago.

America might have turned his head. He might have learned how to be a real lady-killer. He certainly had the looks and the appeal, he just needed the inclination and the desire. The high after a good performance might do it. And she'd virtually shoved him into that woman's arms. He may well separate work and socializing. Tess was work, the BB wasn't.

But what else could she do? Tag along like some sort of sheepdog? It wasn't her style of party; none of the players ever went or were expected to go to those things. David hadn't invited her and Ian had only done so out of embarrassment. Much more dignified to have declined. Out of self-respect.

She wasn't that desperate for David's attention. Where were they?

Just after 1 A.M., a car's lights washed across the blind. Tess sat up, ears straining, hands tensed on the sheet covering her body. Doors slammed, voices called, the engine revved, the lights swept away. Footsteps sounded on the path, up the steps. Laughter. The scratching of a key. Muttered cursing. More laughter, loud and uninhibited followed by a bout of shushing. Stuart's voice. A clatter as keys fell to the stone step.

She sprang out of bed. They were drunk! Both of them. Fumbling about and laughing like a couple of total idiots. She raced to the front door and flung it open. Two startled faces stared at her. Stu was bent over in the act of rescuing his keys, giggling inanely. David leaned against the wall laughing like a loon.

"Aah. Tessie," Stu said, straightening carefully. "Lucky you were home. Did we wake you?"

"No! I was worried sick," she yelled. "I didn't know where you were, either of you."

"We've been celebrating." David smiled cheerfully. She studied him with suspicion. Not drunk, just very relaxed and happy.

"So I see," she said fiercely while relief danced in her chest.

"You didn't want to come," he said.

"Should've come, Tessie," mumbled Stu. He leaned forward, hugged her, and kissed her enthusiastically on the cheek. "Thanks for putting me up. I have to go to bed. I have an early flight." He turned to David and stuck out his hand. "May not see you in the morning. Delighted to meet you. Night all." He released David's hand, pushed his way past Tess and staggered down to his room.

David stepped inside. Tess closed the door and followed him to the family area. He pulled his bowtie from his pocket and removed his jacket.

"You should've come. You're the Party Girl."

"I've changed since then, David. And anyway that was only your idea of me. You decided I was a party girl but you didn't know me at all!" Tess glared at him. "Why doesn't anyone understand? I've changed! I've grown up."

He regarded her thoughtfully. "Not so much."

"I have!" Her fingers curled into fists.

"Why did you kiss me then? In front of Lisa." Lisa?! A smile lurked. Teasing. Horrible man. He was far too handsome standing there in his white dress shirt, top buttons undone, hair mussed. By whom?

"To make you feel good. Why else?"

He shrugged, raised an eyebrow. "I don't know." His gaze traveled up and down her body. Straight out of bed in short pajama pants and a crop top. No robe. Too bad. He'd seen her in a bikini exposing far more skin.

Tess stared back defiantly. "I'm going to bed."

An arm snaked out and dragged her close. His free hand caressed her cheek, slipped around the back of her neck; his mouth closed on hers. This was a proper kiss, one that melted every bone in her body, every nerve, every tendon, and every organ. Both arms wrapped around her and held her up. Her own arms hung loose by her sides, no strength to lift them, all awareness centered on the point of contact, lips, the way his mouth moved on hers, gentle, thorough. Tasting of wine, sweet. And salt. And him. Then he released her. Too soon, way too soon.

"That was to make you feel good," he said blandly.

Tess blinked, surfaced. "I didn't feel bad," she managed to say. Liar.

"Doesn't matter. Made you feel even better, didn't it? Sleep tight." He turned away, slung the jacket over his arm and headed for his bedroom.

Sleep? How could she sleep now? And it seemed she'd seriously underestimated David Montgomery's ability to confuse and confound the opposite sex. He was no nerdy geek unaware of his attractiveness to women. Oh no. He was a real danger and he knew it. He'd learned certain things in America.

Stu had left when Tess hauled herself out of bed in the morning scratchy-eyed and lethargic. A shower helped only marginally. She needed coffee and a sugar hit. Porridge with thick, rich golden syrup.

David looked up from the table where he sat reading the paper. "Good morning." Bright-eyed, friendly. No aftereffects at all. No grudge-holding. Probably slept the sleep of the innocent.

Tess grunted something indeterminate and checked the jug for water. Full, newly boiled.

"Tea's made," he said.

"I want coffee."

He went back to his paper. Tess fumbled about making coffee, spilling grains, spilling hot water, dropping a mug so it shattered on the granite bench with a hideously loud crash.

"Did you cut yourself?" He didn't get up. Mildly interested.

"No." She scraped broken pieces into the bin, used a sponge to clear the fragments.

David folded the paper and stood up. "I'll be off."

Where was he going? Tess took oatmeal from the cupboard and a saucepan. Began making porridge. He went into his room and came out a moment later with a cream linen jacket over his black T-shirt. He looked like a male model. He'd kissed her. Messed with her head. Deliberately? Stinker. He wasn't interested in her in the long term. She was the easy flirt, the Party Girl. Did he think he'd be getting some free favors during the next month? As payback for deceiving him? Was that what that kiss was about? Tess glowered as she stirred the porridge.

"See you later," he said on his way past.

Tess spun around. "Don't think I'll be letting you kiss me whenever you feel like it while you're here."

He frowned and his head jerked back in astonishment. "Why would I think that?"

Tess snorted. "The way you kissed me last night. As though you thought I was easy . . ." She stopped as an unexpected burst of tears dammed themselves up behind her eyes. She swallowed, choked them down, clamping her lips together.

David stared at her, eyes cool. "The last word I associate with you is easy." A tiny smile twisted his mouth. "Put last night down to post-concert euphoria and champagne. Plus Stuart's good company. Don't worry, your virtue is safe with me."

The way he said virtue implied any virtue she'd possessed was long gone. Tess turned back to her porridge, which had begun to stick to the pan and burn. The front door clicked shut.

David checked out more apartments after his meeting with Ian. Hopeless. They were all dismal as Tess had forewarned. He sat in a café in the Chatswood Mall and considered his options over cappuccino and a tomato and basil bruschetta. There was no immediate rush now that the rental issue with Tess was sorted out. Stuart was none the wiser, fortunately. The last thing David wanted to do was stir up trouble, upset the status quo regardless of how annoyed he was with her. Stuart was a nice guy despite his poor and rather biased opinion of his sister and her profession. Not that anyone could blame him given her track record. At one point in the alcohol-sodden night he said she appeared to have settled down since their father's death.

David had had to bite his tongue and it pained him to be part of such a childish deception but Stu went on to say, "It really shook her up. Dad and Tessie never really got their act together. Too similar in temperament. Did nothing but fight. She's never said so but I think she regrets not making her peace with him. In her own weirdo way she's trying to prove something to herself now. Heaven knows what."

"That she can be responsible?" suggested David.

Stuart snorted with laughter. "Tess will never be accused of that." Unfortunately, David had to agree.

The two Japanese businessmen returned from the bar just then with another bottle of champagne and the celebrations rolled on.

David drained the last of the coffee. What he really should do was go to Cootamundra and visit his parents. Four years since he'd seen them. The weekend was free. He could rent a car. A five-hour drive in the Australian countryside would be fun. Escape from the city, from Tess and the tension in the house. He stood up. If he got himself organized he could leave tonight. Be there before twelve. Come back Sunday night.

Tess was practicing when he let himself into the house. Fid galloped down the hall bouncing and springing. Nice to be greeted so warmly. Nonjudgmental, unconditional love. He bent to tousle the soft ears and received a lick on the thumb. The familiar pong lingered in the family area. Still hadn't properly laid eyes on the Phantom, just heard snuffling noises from his kennel in the dark. He took the phone and phone book and went to sit on the terrace in fresher air. Rental cars. Quite a choice. He dialed.

Tess went to the kitchen. David heard the fridge open and close. Footsteps came toward the terrace. She sat down opposite holding a glass of water.

"I want a car for the weekend, please."

Tess frowned. "Where are you going?"

"Cootamundra," he mouthed as the rental car woman began asking what sort of car he wanted.

"Take the Diva."

The Diva? "Just a moment, please." He put his hand over the receiver. "What did you say?"

"Take the Diva," she said.

"To Cootamundra?"

She nodded. He said into the phone, "I'm sorry, I'll have to call back." To Tess, "I can't do that. What about you?"

"I'm not going anywhere."

"But it's your car."

"I know. But as you said, you're helping me pay for it." She regarded him intently, paused, working herself up to say something. "I feel—I owe you for"—she stretched her mouth in a grimace—"you know . . ."

"You don't have to lend me your car."

"I want to."

Tempting. Extremely tempting. She did owe him. Big time. And that car would be something else out on the open road.

"The Diva needs a good run and she's great on the freeway. How long does it take?"

"Five hours."

She grinned that cheeky grin of hers. Her eyes sparkled. "You'll do it in four."

"I will not! I'm a very responsible driver."

"I know or I wouldn't offer her. So does that mean you'll accept?"

David considered for a split second. How impressed would his dad the mechanic be? What a ride he'd have. "Yes. Thank you. I'd like to leave this evening."

"Fine. Whenever you like."

An hour later he was on the road, overnight bag and violin on the backseat, Tess' opera arias in the CD player, the Diva chomping at the bit as they entered the harbor tunnel heading for the M5 and the Hume Highway to the vast southwest.

The weekend dragged. Leaden. Tess took Fid for a walk after David drove decorously down the street in the Diva. At that rate he'd have to turn around and come back as soon as he arrived.

She woke way too early the next morning and lay in bed watching the light gather strength outside. Had he arrived safely? Must have or she'd know. The Diva was registered in her name. In an accident they'd check with her. Accident? What was she thinking? David was the least likely person to smash up the Diva she could possibly think of, herself included. And if he did, she'd kill him! If he hadn't already killed himself, in which case . . . For goodness' sake!

Tess clambered out of bed. Ridiculous. She had to go

to Tai Chi. Maria from class was picking her up in twenty minutes. The meditation was exactly what she needed and the concentration required to do the movements would take her mind off David for at least an hour.

After class and breakfast the whole Saturday stretched before her. Empty. Stuart phoned sometime in the endless morning thanking her for the room, etcetera, saying how much he liked David. How surprised he was she had a friend like that.

"How rude is that?" she cried.

"Well, most of your friends are complete losers, you must admit," he said with a laugh.

"What about Lauren? You like her. You even wanted to date her except she thought *you* were the loser when we were at school."

"I said most. How is the luscious Lauren?"

"Overseas. I miss her."

"Me too.

"Oh shut up, Stu." Tess laughed despite the rankling annoyance at his constant dismissal of her life.

"Gotta go. Love you, Tessie."

"You too. Bye." And it was true. She did love Stu. He was all she had in the way of meaningful family. Who knew where their mother was? And Uncle Edgar, Dad's brother, was alive but had lost touch years ago. A bitter fraternal feud meant the brothers hadn't spoken since the age of twenty-three, although Edgar and Aunt Celia did appear at the funeral. Cousins Susan,

Mandy, and Fiona lived their own lives in other cities. The Fullers weren't a close-knit bunch. Not like the Montgomerys.

Aaron rang and invited her to a lunchtime barbecue the following day. She accepted with the proviso that she be home by five. In case David came home earlier than expected. What had she done before he came to stay? Practiced? Walked Fid? Shopped? Were her free days always as empty and she just hadn't noticed?

She didn't enjoy the outing with Aaron. It filled in time, that was the best to be said about it. His jokes and loud good humor that previously had seemed fun began to grate. The crazy antics of his friends as they celebrated a mate's thirtieth birthday at a pool party suddenly seemed childish and silly. Even boring.

At four she pleaded a headache, refused Aaron's offer to drive her home and insisting he stay and enjoy himself, and instead she called a taxi. David wouldn't be home yet, far too early. He'd want to spend as much time with his family as possible. She could understand that in theory if not in practice. He'd mentioned he hadn't seen his parents for four years. They'd spoken often on the phone but it was clear he missed them and eagerly looked forward to the visit. He probably wouldn't leave till about five or six at the latest.

At five she fed the dogs. At seven she began preparing a pasta sauce and put a saucepan of water on to boil. At ten past seven the phone rang.

"Hello." Light and hopeful. David, telling her he was on his way. Coming home to her.

"Is that Theresa Anne Fuller?"

"Yes."

"Constable Ivan Bobolas, Yass Police. Are you the registered owner of a Mercedes sports car, NSW registration . . ." Her mind barely took in the details of the numbers he read out. David?

"Yes, yes I am. What's happened?" Breath came in short shallow gasps. Her heart thumped so loudly she could barely hear his voice. She leaned against the bench as her legs suddenly gave way. "David, where's David?"

"I'm sorry, ma'am. There's been an accident . . ."

Her spine snapped upright. "No, that's impossible. David wouldn't have an accident," she said loudly. Stupid policeman, didn't he know? David was a good, careful driver.

"I'm sorry, there's been an accident," he repeated. "The car rolled and was hit by a semitrailer. Mr. Montgomery has been taken to Yass District Hospital."

"A semitrailer!" Must be alive, *must* be or he would have said. The other was inconceivable. Injured, then. How badly? Hit by a semi?!

"He's alive and hasn't broken anything as far as I can tell. He got out of the car before the semi hit it, but sustained a blow to the head from something flying about loose in the car."

"Did you see him? Were you there?"

"I arrived at the scene about ten minutes after the

call came in. The truckie was very shaken up, thought the car driver had been killed. But we found Mr. Montgomery sitting by the roadside. He was in shock. Disoriented. If he hadn't been in such a safe car it would've been far worse. He was able to get out by himself. The truckie said the car was on its roof in the middle of the road when he came round the bend. Had no time to brake or swerve without jack-knifing the rig. He had a load of cattle."

Tess listened but didn't comprehend much. The only words that registered were "alive" and "uninjured." Alive. He was alive. Of course he'd be in shock. Then questions flooded her brain. How? What we were the circumstances? What about his violin? "Why did he crash? Did he skid? Was someone overtaking, on his side of the road?"

"There were no witnesses. No real telling what happened but there are a lot of roos in the area and there was blood and fur on the front bumper."

"Can't he tell you?"

"He's not making much sense. Can't remember the accident."

"Can't remember?" A blow to the head, he'd said. Amnesia?

"You'll need to speak to the doctors."

Tess groped for some sense in the mess of information, all of it incomprehensible. Someone else. He must be talking about some other David Montgomery. "He's only been back in Australia for a week," she said.

"He has a Californian license." It *was* the same David. Her David.

"Yes, he checked it was legal to drive with it. It is legal, isn't it?"

"Yes. For three months. Important for your insurance claim."

Insurance? Realization slammed in. The Diva. Smashed by a truck. And David hurt, in pain. With amnesia. Too much. She sank to the floor clutching the phone to her ear with fingers so tense they hurt. "What should I do?"

"Nothing you can do at the moment. I can organize the car to be towed to Yass where your insurance company will want to assess the damage. It'll be a write-off. No hope of repairing it." Stated with such matter-of-fact calm.

"A write-off?" But what about David?

"They'll pay out in full." He thought she didn't understand. She didn't. Nothing made sense.

"When can he come home? Should I go to Yass to be with him?"

"Are you his wife?"

"No. I'm—I'm a friend. He shares the house." And then another realization. "His parents, he was visiting his parents in Cootamundra."

"Do you have an address?"

"No, I'm sorry." Her face was wet, her neck. Tears streaming down her cheeks, unheeded till now. "But he left a phone number. Wait." She rose unsteadily and scrabbled about in the mess of paper on the bench for the neatly written contact number, read it out. "Will you phone them or should I?"

"Whatever you'd prefer. Sometimes the news is better coming from a friend rather than from us."

"Oh, no. I'm not—I don't know them. I don't know what to do," she wailed.

"In that case perhaps I should call them."

"Yes, please, maybe that would be best. Tell them— tell them to call me if they want to. All his things are here. Tell them they can stay here if they come to Sydney. Tell them . . ." She stopped, groped blindly for the tea towel, and mopped her eyes as best she could one handed.

"Perhaps you can tell them yourself," he said gently. "I'll give them your number."

"Yes. Please. I'm sorry." Subdued now. Deflated.

"That's quite all right, Miss Fuller. I understand. You make yourself a nice hot cup of tea and try not to worry. This is the number of the Yass Hospital. They'll tell you what's happening."

"Thank you. Thank you very much. Just one more thing—did he have his violin with him? It's very valuable, David's a violinist."

"Yes. He was clutching the case when we found him but he didn't seem to know why or what it was."

As soon as he disconnected Tess pressed the numbers for the hospital with shaking fingers. Wrong. Someone with a strong foreign accent answered. Tried again. This time she got Yass Hospital reception.

"Yes, David Montgomery has been admitted. He's undergoing a preliminary examination but will probably be transferred to Canberra Hospital either tonight or in the morning depending on when they can admit him."

"Can I speak to a doctor, please?"

"Are you a relative?"

"No—a—a friend."

"I'm sorry we can't give information to nonrelatives."

"But he's not in any danger?"

The nurse laughed comfortably. "No, don't worry, he's not going to die."

"Why does he need to be transferred?"

"We don't have the specialists here."

"Specialists for what?"

"He needs to undergo further neurological testing. It's standard for injuries of this kind. He sustained a blow to the head."

"Oh."

"You should contact his family."

"Have they called?"

"Not yet."

Tess hung up in a fever of impatience and indecision. What if David's parents didn't call her? Why should they? They may not even know she existed. But they must. David was driving her car and being scrupulously honest he'd never pretend the Diva was his. But he might simply say it belonged to a friend. But he was living with her.

What to do? She had no idea.

The water on the stove was bubbling furiously so she went to turn it off. No appetite. And what about the Diva? The nice policeman had said make a hot cup of tea. No— a nice cup of tea. He was nice—nice cop, nice tea. How could she not worry? He didn't say how. She was raving.

Tess spooned tea leaves into the pot with great concentration and poured in the water from the saucepan. No teabags, David hated them. He liked his tea made properly. So did she.

Hot tea. Good for shock. He had amnesia, someone said—the policeman. No, couldn't remember the accident. Disoriented. Neurological tests. Precautionary, that's what they'd be. Being thorough, checking everything.

The phone rang while she was drinking her tea, laced with sugar because she thought that was supposed to be good for shock too. She pounced on it.

"Hello."

"Is that Tess?" A woman. His mother?

"Yes. Mrs. Montgomery?" she cried eagerly.

"Yes. Please call me Joyce. You've heard about the accident?" She spoke calmly, matter-of-factly as though she were asking if Tess had seen the latest movie.

By contrast Tess babbled, the words pouring out in an unstoppable flow. "Yes, the police rang a while ago. I'm so worried—I phoned the hospital but they wouldn't tell me anything except he has to go to Canberra Hospital for tests. But they said that was standard. Neurological tests. He can't remember the accident."

Joyce again, calm and soothing. "That's right. They're worried about the blow to the head." Now her voice shook a little. "I think it must have been my pot of honey. We keep bees, you see, and I'd sent a jar home with him. For you both."

"For me?" Breathless with astonishment. For them both. Like a couple.

"I thought you'd like it. Fresh from . . . I'm sorry Tess. I'm rambling from the shock." She dragged in air, her breath audible through the phone line. Someone murmured in the background. His father? "He's all right they say. No broken bones, no injuries apart from the honey pot." She paused then blurted, "I feel so guilty about that."

"No, don't! The policeman said he thought he must have hit a kangaroo. David wouldn't be expecting that any more, having been in America so long. Anybody can hit a kangaroo."

"That's true, the mad things."

A pause. Joyce's breath feathered into the phone.

Tess said, "Will you go to Canberra if they take him there?"

"Yes, it's only a two-hour drive. We'll go across tomorrow."

"I don't know if I should come too."

"You don't need to, darl."

"But my car . . ."

"Doug can take care of all that for you. He knows

the trade." David's dad? Why would he help her, a girl he didn't know, someone who'd taken advantage of his son? Deceived him in a selfish way these people couldn't comprehend. Such a self-serving action wouldn't be within their consciousness.

"Would he do that?"

"Of course! We own a garage, didn't David tell you? Doug deals with that type of thing all the time. He knows all the tow truck drivers and mechanics in the area. You just need to contact your insurance company."

"Well . . . if it's no trouble . . . I'd be so grateful. I don't think I could bear to see my car all smashed up."

"I understand. You were very generous to loan it to him. The police told us that if he'd been in anything less safe he'd probably have been killed or at least very badly injured. It's such a shame you've lost that beautiful car. He'll be very upset about it."

"I don't care," said Tess vehemently. "I don't care about the car. I just want him to be safe." And it was true. All in a rush the reality of the statement hit her. She didn't care about the Diva. David's health and well-being were paramount. She loved him with every fiber of her being. The thought of him being injured was a gaping hole in her core. "I think I will come to Canberra. I'll fly down. I can bring some of his things with me. He'll need more clothes."

"All right, darl. And can you tell the orchestra? We've no idea who to call."

"Of course."

Ian was horrified when Tess spoke to him shortly after finishing her talk with Joyce.

"I'll need a few days off, Ian," she said. "I'll ring you tomorrow when I find out something. It sounds as though he's physically all right, thank goodness. But he'll need some time to recover."

"Whatever it takes, Tess. We can cover you both. Give him our best wishes for a speedy recovery."

"Of course."

Then she fired up the computer and booked herself a one-way ticket to Canberra leaving midmorning.

"Neurology ward. Just past the cafeteria and through the doors," the receptionist said pointing across the wide foyer. "He's in bed four."

Tess followed the directions but hesitated at the door to the room. People were in there, clustered about the bed. His parents? The man glanced up and saw her hovering.

"Are you Tess?" The tanned, weatherbeaten face had David's smile and David's eyes. So familiar, so kindly but shadowed at the moment with concern.

"Yes." She stepped forward.

The woman, square-shouldered and graying, turned with a gasp and a smile. She held out her arms. "Hello, darl, I'm so glad you've come." To Tess' amazement, tears streamed down her cheeks but before she could utter a word she was enveloped in a warm hug and kissed soundly on the cheek. Joyce held her arm snugly as she drew her toward the bed. "Maybe he'll remember you."

"Remember me?" Tess' gaze flew to the figure in the bed. He looked remarkably fine. No bandages, rather pale but more or less the same as when she'd waved him good-bye on Friday evening. So long ago. Her lips wobbled as she smiled but he didn't smile in return.

"Hello, David." Tess moved closer, bent down to kiss him. He drew back, turning his head away, frowning.

"I'm sorry," he said in that familiar voice. "I don't know who you are."

Chapter Eight

"I'm Tess." She looked at his parents in bewilderment, gulped back tears. Amnesia? The policeman said he couldn't remember the accident but not that he couldn't remember *anything*.

"He doesn't remember us either," said his father. Joyce gave a convulsive sob and grabbed Tess' arm again.

"We were hoping he'd recognize you," she said.

Tess' eyes flew to David and a groundswell of fear rose from deep within. "He doesn't." She bit at her lip to prevent the tears from cascading down her cheeks. Lost already and only just found. Her love. But not his. Never his now.

His voice startled her. "I don't know anyone. Apparently Doug and Joyce are my parents." He stared at her. "I might know you. I don't know."

Tess said, "You're living in my house at the moment—in Balmoral. In Sydney."

"Am I?"

"You're a violinist and I'm a viola player. We work in the City Symphony Orchestra. You've just arrived from America to become the new concert master."

He continued to stare at her with a slightly puzzled expression. "That's what they told me."

"Don't you remember anything?"

He shook his head slowly.

Doug said, "The doctor told us this might only last a few days."

"Or months or even years," added Joyce.

He ignored her and went on. "Memories can filter back in slowly and sometimes something can trigger a whole avalanche and it all comes back in a rush. Other times parts of the memory stay blank forever."

"In other words," put in David, "they don't know."

"But there is a chance this won't last long at all?" Tess grasped eagerly at the slim straw of hope.

"So the doc says," agreed Doug.

"So he should come home to Sydney where he was living and see if something clicks."

"We thought taking him home to Cootamundra might be best. He grew up there." A hint of steel glimmered in Joyce's tone. Protecting her child. As a mother should. Not like Tess' mother.

"Oh, uh—yes. I suppose. Except he hadn't been there for years and his violin was his whole life. His music is in Sydney. So is the orchestra." *And me*, she screamed silently. Who was she to come between mother and son?

David said nothing, watching. Joyce exchanged a long look with her husband. He raised his eyebrows in exactly the way David did. "She's right, love," he said. "David said the place had changed so much he didn't recognize it. We're not even in the same house anymore."

Joyce sighed long, slow and defeated. "We haven't seen him for years and now . . . I just want my David back." She burrowed in her pocket and produced a tissue to blow her nose.

"So do I," said Tess.

"Come and have a cuppa, love," said Doug. "Leave Tess and David alone for a bit."

"They seem very nice people," David said after they'd left the room.

"Yes they do."

"Don't you know them either?"

"No. I've never met them."

He was staring at her again. "Tell me, Tess. What sort of relationship did we have? Do we have? I mean, why was I staying with you?"

Tess ran her tongue over lips, suddenly dry. The hospital was very warm. She removed her jacket. If he truly remembered nothing, the full and unvarnished truth would help no one. "You were staying with me for a month while you looked for your own place. It was meant to be just a week but you decided to stay on longer."

"Why?"

She met his curious gaze. "We were students together in Canberra. Eleven years ago. You're older by a couple of years. And you like my house. It's big and it's near the beach. You like to swim and surf."

"So we're old friends." He drew in a deep breath, seemed happy with that bit of information. "Are we or were we more than friends?"

The question came suddenly, taking her by surprise. Her face prickled uncomfortably with a heated rush of blood.

"Sorry if that embarrasses you." He leaned forward earnestly, sitting up in the bed. "But you've no idea what it's like to . . . to not know who you are, not even know your parents. I need to learn as much as I can about myself. Who I am. Who I was."

She swallowed. "I've always loved you," she said softly.

"Do I love you?"

She looked at her fingers, twisting around each other so her rings dug in and the joints were white from the pressure. Couldn't lie. Not about this. "I don't know. You've never said."

He smiled slowly as he sank back against the pillows. "I should love you. You're the most beautiful girl I've ever seen." He paused and frowned. "I think." The smile lurked again. "No, I can definitively say you're the most beautiful girl I can ever remember seeing."

Tess smiled. "You've never told me that before."

He laughed and it took all her willpower not to climb into the bed with him. "I must have been mad."

"You were always completely focused on music."

"Always?"

Tess nodded. "To the exclusion of all else."

"What a crashing bore I must have been."

"I never thought you were boring but . . ."

"But?"

"It was very frustrating."

"Well, maybe we can remedy that." His eyes targeted hers, direct and provocative. David's eyes but not David. Unsettling. Exciting.

"How long will you be in here?"

"They're waiting for some test results. To see if I have a brain." He laughed again.

"Do you have any other injuries apart from your head?"

"A bruised hip and shoulder from the seat belt." He grimaced. "Sorry about your car. They tell me it's totaled."

Tess nodded, unable to speak. The casual tone hurt more than she expected. He didn't know what he was talking about, she must remember that. He didn't remember anything, only what he'd been told. It wouldn't seem real. He didn't remember the Diva.

"What sort of car was it?"

"A Mercedes sports. Silver."

He shrugged lightly. "Sorry, that means nothing. Was it expensive?" The brown eyes met hers. Strangely distant. Polite.

She held his gaze. "Very. I called her the Diva."

"The Diva," he said thoughtfully.

"Yes." Tess waited as he pondered the term. Remembering?

"Is a diva a singer?"

"Yes." A sigh of disappointment. "A female singer with class. A prima donna."

"Sorry."

"You're alive, that's the main thing," she said.

When Joyce and Doug came back from their tea break David said, "I'd like to go to Sydney with Tess. If that's where I was living I've more chance of remembering, I think."

David clipped his seat belt in the rear seat of the taxi. Tess spoke to the driver, giving him directions to somewhere called Balmoral where he gathered they lived. He only had her word for it, of course. Any of it. But as he couldn't remember any other reality this one may as well do. Tess was an absolute stunner and if she wanted to take him home with her—why object? Where else would he go? To that place called Cootamundra with the nice, friendly, worried couple who judging by the photos they'd shown him were his parents? Tess won hands down.

Bright glittering sun streamed onto his face. He patted his pocket for sunglasses. Not there. "Do I own sunglasses?" he asked Tess.

"Yes. Maybe you left them in the Diva."

"Maybe. It's warmer here than in Canberra, isn't it?"

"Yes. It's farther north."

He peered out the window, searching for something familiar. Everywhere they'd been he scanned the surroundings hopefully. The drive from the hospital to the airport in Canberra. Nothing. Tess even asked the taxi driver to detour by the School of Music but the big concrete building with its odd bunkerlike architecture struck no chord.

The short plane ride seemed familiar in the way cars seemed familiar. He didn't have to think about where to stow the overnight bag and his violin, just reached up and shoved them into the overhead locker, then sat and clipped his seat belt without thinking too, the same as he'd done in the taxi just now. The doctor had explained that different parts of the brain controlled different aspects of memory so that while he couldn't remember people and events, automatic functions like speech, eating, and walking weren't affected. "You'll still be able to ride a bike, swim, and play the violin," he'd said. "That's if you could do them before."

"At the same time?" David had asked, making the doctor laugh.

Tess said, "Does this look familiar?" Glimpses of a gigantic arching gray bridge flashed between the buildings ahead of them.

"Wow," he said. "What is it?"

"The Sydney Harbour Bridge and there's the Opera House." She pointed to the right as they swung up onto the approach to the bridge. An extraordinary white building sat on a little promontory jutting into the harbor. Big, shell-shaped structures formed the roof, sparkling in the brilliant sunlight. "You played the Beethoven Violin Concerto in there the day before your accident. I played in the orchestra."

David stared at the building willing himself to remember such a momentous occasion. "Was that the first time I'd played there?"

"Yes, I think so. It was very important to you. You'd always wanted to perform the Beethoven as leader of the City Symphony. You told me it was something you'd dreamed of since you were a child."

The thick gray struts of the bridge obscured the Opera House as the taxi crossed the harbor but the view was still magnificent. The water stretched away to the left and right busy with ferries, yachts, a large tanker, and an old-fashioned replica sailing ship. Skyscrapers crowded the foreshore but houses were nestled in among trees and greenery as well, some with lawns reaching down to the rocky shoreline.

Nothing looked familiar. Try as he might nothing sprang out and said, "Remember me."

The taxi finally stopped in a tree-lined hilly street outside a house almost completely obscured by trees and shrubbery. Tess paid the driver and they stood holding their overnight bags while the taxi drove away. The violin was heavy in his hand but the weight felt familiar.

"Anything?" she asked.

"No."

Tess pushed the gate open and strode along a little stone path and up three steps to the front door. A floral perfume wafted into his nostrils—something familiar. Just couldn't quite . . . it was gone. She shoved in a key and darted inside to press buttons on a key pad just inside the door.

"Tchaikovsky," he said suddenly.

Tess' head snapped around. "Eighteen Twelve Overture." A grin split her face. "You remember the code?"

"No. It just sprang into my head for some reason when I watched you do that."

"It was easy for me to remember," she said.

"Do you forget things?" He followed her down the corridor glancing into side rooms as they went. A beautiful house. No wonder he'd decided to stay here. With the lovely Tess in residence as well. He hadn't been a complete loser despite being a bore.

"Not really. I can be a bit scatterbrained." She dumped her bag on the floor of a spacious sitting room with big glass doors opening onto a patio and garden. A little brown-and-white dog stared in at them wagging his tail frantically.

David dropped his bag next to hers, placed his violin on the table, and walked across to open the door. The dog leaped on him with delight, wriggling his whole body and licking any part of David's anatomy within range of his tongue.

"Hello, boy! What's your name?" He tousled the ears and patted the small excited body.

"Fidelio. Fid," called Tess. The dog left him and scampered to her side to repeat the licking and wiggling routine.

"Friendly dog."

"You and he get on very well. You took him for walks. We have another dog too. He's very old. Hannibal. He's a dear but very slow and he has a few medical problems."

David nodded. He wasn't sure if he liked dogs or not. This little one certainly liked him. Tess shooed the dog out and closed the door.

"Where's my room?"

"Through here." Tess opened a door to a short passageway. The bedroom she showed him was painted pale lavender gray. Very restful with a lovely view of the garden and in the distance, the harbor. She'd brought his violin in with her and placed it on the bed.

David studied the case. Sturdy, black with an identification tag and some travel stickers on it. Tess clicked the lid open and the violin lay exposed. He hadn't even ventured to open the case. A hospital didn't seem to be the right scenario to try something so deeply personal. They'd all assured him it had been his life, that his existence had been centered around the instrument hidden in that case. He'd taken it from the overturned car without knowing. An automatic response. What if he couldn't play despite what the doctor had said? What would his life mean then?

"Play it," she said.

"I don't know . . ." He glanced at her for encouragement and she nodded. He reached out a hand tentatively and grasped the violin by the neck. Tess handed him the bow. Something took over then. He tucked the instrument snugly under his chin and the feeling was so familiar he smiled. He *did* know how to play. Somehow he just knew he did.

He stroked the bow across the strings and winced, adjusted the fine-tuning. Tried again. Better. Another slight adjustment of the E string. Perfect. He began to play. The music poured from the violin as if he was channeling it with no control over the source. He had no idea where it came from. His subconscious?

Tess stood there smiling with her hands clasped in front of her. "Do you remember?" Those lovely eyes shone wide with excitement and a sheen of tears.

He stopped and shook his head. Hated to disappoint her. "What am I playing?"

"The last movement of the Beethoven Violin Concerto."

"Amazing. I have no idea what I'm playing but it just comes out."

"You played by memory so I suppose it's in your muscles like the doctor said. It's automatic."

He laid the violin carefully back in its case. "I wonder what else I can do."

"You can swim. I've seen you. Would you like to walk down to the beach?"

"Maybe later. I'm a bit tired now and my head's aching."

"Sorry. You have a rest. I'll make you a cup of tea." She backed out hastily. David sat on the bed and gazed around the room. His room. That must be his robe hanging on the back of the door and his black shoes sitting neatly on the floor by the wardrobe. He walked across and opened the doors. Shirts, T-shirts, slacks, a dinner suit, and a couple of jackets. Predominantly white, blue, and black. Jeans. Conservative. Runners on the floor, sandals and a pair of slip-ons similar to the ones he wore except they were dark brown rather than black.

He pulled open the drawers of the dressing table one by one and studied the contents. Underwear. Socks. Papers. He took these out and flipped through them. His contract with the orchestra, letters from someone called Ian Moore, orchestral manager. A passport—his. Photos in an envelope.

David sat on one of the chairs in the bay window to look carefully at each one. A group of smiling people sitting around an outdoor table. He sat at one end with a glass of wine and a big grin. Not one face was familiar. Himself with a surfboard and a tan at a beach somewhere. Must be able to surf. More groups of people, some including him, some not. A string quartet in performance. Ravel. The name popped into his head as he looked at the photo. Did Ravel write a string quartet? Tess would know.

As if on cue she tapped on the door holding a mug in one hand.

"Did Ravel write a string quartet?" He held up the photo.

"Yes." Tess exchanged the mug for the photo. "This must have been just before you left America for here. See the date? August. Maybe it was at a summer music festival."

He put the tea down on the small table. "Maybe we'll never know." He slipped the picture back into the envelope with the other useless photographs of the life that was once his and was now as foreign to him as that of the ancient Egyptians. Unless he knew a lot about them. Who knew? He tossed the envelope onto the table.

"It'll come back to you, David," Tess said earnestly. "Parts of it already are."

"What parts?" Depression bit suddenly, hard and deep. The bump on his head throbbed painfully.

"You remembered the alarm code and Ravel, and you played your violin perfectly."

"I didn't remember anything, Tess. I didn't even know I could play the violin and I'd hardly say I remembered the alarm code." Her optimism was touching but completely unfounded.

"But do you remember it now?"

"Eighteen twelve," he said.

"See!"

Wow, her smile was glorious. Pity he didn't share her enthusiasm.

"I can remember things after the accident," he pointed out morosely.

"And you'll remember things before. We just have to find a trigger."

He met her eyes. "We? Why would you bother? From what you've said we haven't seen each other for years and I've only been here a week. We hardly know each other. I certainly don't know you." He gave a humorless snort of laughter.

She bit her lip and the light dimmed in her face. That was unnecessarily cruel but he couldn't help it. "I'm sorry. It's just so frustrating . . ." He stood up and turned his back on her disappointment, stared out at the peaceful green of the garden. A large black dog staggered past the window. Decrepit. Very gray around the ears and muzzle. So old it could barely put one paw in front of the other.

"That's Hannibal."

"Yes," she cried with such delight he couldn't stand it.

"You told me before," he said harshly. "When we came in."

"Oh." So crestfallen.

He turned to face her. Curiosity overcame the anger, the urge to crush her childish belief that he would suddenly and miraculously regain his identity. "Why do you care?"

She looked him straight in the eye. "I love you."

"So you said. But why? What is it about me you love?"

"I always had a tremendous crush on you when we were students but you were always very intent on your studies and never socialized with the rest of us. I thought you were the best-looking guy I'd ever seen," she said with a tiny grin. "I still do." She sat down on one of the easy chairs. "When Ian asked if you could stay here for a while I was interested to see if I still felt the same way. I did, do." She paused, stretched out her legs, glanced down at her bare feet sporting pink toenails. "And so do you."

"Meaning?"

"You never took any notice of any of the girls when we were students."

"I'm not gay, am I?" The way he felt when she was around he doubted that very much.

She laughed. "No."

"But why? Why do you love me?"

Her cheeks deepened to a rosy pink. He stepped toward her and touched a finger to her chin. All irritation fled replaced by rising desire.

"I really want to know, Tess. I don't know what sort of person I am. If someone like you loves me it tells me I can't be a complete dead loss."

"Someone like me?" Her voice caught in her throat.

He nodded. "Someone as beautiful and caring and sensitive as you."

She gazed up at him without speaking. Tess was

beautiful. He loved her. Overwhelmingly. He knew it. But was it a new infatuation or one of long-standing? Was it the result of the insecurity of his present situation? Was he attaching himself to her as a lost puppy would? Or was it just hormones? He had no way of judging. His yardsticks were gone in the fog. Tread carefully.

Her voice came softly, husky with emotion. "I love you because you're strong. You're decent and good and you follow your own path. I admire that in you. You have a sense of yourself that I've never had. Now I've met your parents I can see why."

"You seem very capable and strong to me."

She shook her head and the wild mane of hair bounced about her face. "I'm not. Not like you."

"I think you are."

He took her hands in his, lifted her so she stood before him, hesitated very briefly but the urge was too strong—he touched his lips to hers. She sighed. Her eyes were closed when he drew away. "I'm not sure I did that properly," he whispered.

Tess slipped her arms around his neck. "Better try again," she murmured.

So he did. And not carefully. He kissed her with abandon and a great sense of release as though this were something he'd wanted to do for a long time but for some inexplicable reason, hadn't. The way she kissed him implied he was correct.

But she was the one to pull away. "I don't think this

is right," she said softly. Her lips were too close and too inviting. He kissed her again. Only token resistance. Oh it was right, very right.

She pressed her hands against his chest. "Why?" he asked.

"Because you're not really you at the moment."

"Do you love this version of me?" He held her against his body.

"Yes, of course I do."

"Well this me wants to kiss you."

To his surprise her eyes filled with tears. He kissed each one gently, tasting salt on his lips. "Why tears?" he murmured.

"Because I've longed to kiss you properly; I've wanted so much to hear you say you do too and now that you have it's . . . it's not really you saying it or you doing it."

"It is me."

She shook her head. "The other David never said anything about how he felt about me."

"He should have."

She didn't reply, just stared into his eyes as if searching for someone else. Someone she knew.

"Tess, what if I never recover my memory?" He placed a finger against her lips as she started to object. "What if this me is the only one there is from now on? Will you believe him if he says he loves you?"

"I want to. But it's too sudden. You've only known me a day or two." Her face twisted in confusion. "I don't know . . . it's just . . . it seems . . . too good to be true."

"That I should love you?" He laughed. "I would think it was the other way around. I'm amazed a girl like you would fall in love with me. How long did it take?"

"For me to fall in love with you?" He nodded. Tess smiled. "About five minutes."

"I rest my case." He planted another quick kiss on her laughing mouth before she could object. "You're gorgeous and desirable and incredibly sexy and I have this really strong, deep feeling I know you. The more time I spend with you the stronger it is."

"But you don't know me at all."

"I know plenty." He knew he wanted to touch her at every opportunity, that he wanted her to smile for him. The wonderful wide smile that made her eyes sparkle.

The worried looked again. "Give it more time, please, David, for my sake?"

He sighed ostentatiously. "For you, I'd do anything."

She stepped away from him, hurriedly and with an obvious anxiety to change the subject. "Have a rest then walk down to the beach with me." Her voice sounded strained. "Tomorrow we'll go to a rehearsal of the orchestra."

That brought him up short. "I can't play with them!"

"No, I know. No one's expecting you to. You've been in a serious accident apart from anything else. You need to rest and recover."

She'd effectively stymied the rampaging desire. His head still pulsed gently at the site of the lump raised by Joyce's pot of honey, reminding him of aches and pains and a great weariness. "Okay. I will lie down for a while."

Tess closed the door as she left. Her heart was thumping so hard it was a miracle he didn't hear it. Pounding away like a sledgehammer. The doctor said mood swings were part of the condition. But this?! This David Montgomery was the man she'd fantasized about as a student but he wasn't the man she loved. Or was he? She did love him, couldn't imagine not loving him, but the man in that room was almost a stranger. Her David wouldn't dream of acting so aggressively, so blatantly suggestively. Except this *was* David.

Too confusing.

Tess went to the study and closed the door. She sat in her father's big leather swivel chair. How easy it would have been to give way to the craving of her body but how wrong it felt. Like taking advantage of him when he was at his most vulnerable. He needed help, not abandoned kisses. Tess smiled wryly. Who'd believe it of Tess Fuller, irresponsible hell-raiser? Party Girl. Turn down a romp with a handsome man, one she was in love with? Unheard of.

She stood up and unpacked her viola. Time to practice. He may not be up to a rehearsal tomorrow but she had a position to fill and notes to perfect.

David wore shorts and sandals at Tess' suggestion. "So as we paddle," she said, "you might remember the feel of the water. Or the sand."

She glanced at him occasionally on the walk to the beach hoping something would click, some sight or sound, the warmth of the sun on his cheek, or the breeze lifting the hair from his brow. He gazed about silently, sniffing the air with an intense concentration as they passed gardens thick with shrubs and flowers.

"That perfume," he said suddenly. "I know that. What is it?"

"Jasmine. A climber." She pointed at the profusion of creamy white flowers trailing over a fence across the road.

"I think it grows at my grandmother's house in Albury."

"You have a grandmother in Albury?" asked Tess eagerly.

He looked down at her, smiling. "I think so. It just came to me."

"Great! They said smell was the closest—or shortest—synaptic leap of any of the senses to the memory. Something scientific like that anyway. You're more likely to remember a smell and associate it with something."

"Perhaps I'd better go round sniffing at things," he said with a sly grin. "I'll start with you." He slung his arm over her shoulder and nuzzled her neck.

"You already smelled me and it didn't remind you of anything," she said, giggling despite her misgivings. This David *was* much more fun and very difficult to resist. Self-denial had never been one of her virtues.

"It does now."

"Just behave yourself," she said sternly, twisting away to walk on.

"Wow! What a view!"

Tess watched his face as he stared out across the bay sparkling in the sunlight under the clear blue sky. He didn't remember any of it, she could tell. Nothing jolted that switch in his brain. Not the bracing salt-laden air close to the water, not the hot sand when they took off their sandals and walked to the gentle waves lapping the beach. Nothing.

"Have I been here often?" The brown eyes swung toward her crinkled against the glare. He'd need new sunglasses. She could've loaned him a pair. Didn't think.

"We swam once and you ran here with Stu—he's my brother—a couple of days ago. You walked down with Fid."

David stood with his hands on his hips staring out over the water. "No wonder I decided to stay with you."

"You told me you like the beach," said Tess.

"That hasn't changed." He faced her, smiling.

They walked home licking gelato in wafer cones. David didn't know if he liked vanilla, chocolate, lemon, or any of the other flavors on offer at the gelato bar so they chose a mix and shared.

"Seems I like everything," he said. "But lemon sorbet is best. Tangy rather than sweet."

"I'm a chocoholic but I restrain myself or I'd be a real bloater."

He let her walk on ahead a few paces. "Impossible."

"Stop ogling. It's true."

"I'm not ogling, I'm admiring. You have a very attractive rear view."

Tess studiously licked her gelato. This was worse than the silent, secret adoration she'd had to practice, wondering if he would ever notice her and resigned to the fact she wasn't his type of girl at all. Or, when he finally did realize she existed wondering would he treat her as anything other than a friend. And that friendship had proven rocky at best. This blatant admiration and flirting was uncomfortable. It wasn't real. She didn't know how to deal with this David, which was weird because coming from any other man she'd have no problem at all.

He needed protecting from himself. What if—and this was an especially frightening thought—his loosened inhibitions applied to any woman? The overtly interested blonde of the concert evening, for example. The way he was carrying on at the moment she'd have him for breakfast, lunch, and dinner.

David went to his room after lunch to sleep. The walk in the hot sun combined with the hill coming home had worn him out. He was still an invalid, Tess reminded him when he admitted how tired he was. She'd keep the dogs out of the house for a week or so until he settled in.

She rang the insurance company about the Diva. They took the name of the garage in Yass where Doug had organized for the twisted wreckage to be towed and said an assessor would check the damage. Then she phoned

Joyce in Cootamundra to give the first of the regular reports she'd promised.

"He's sleeping," Tess said. "I think his head aches a lot and he gets very tired. We walked to the beach this morning."

"Has he remembered anything?"

"Little things pop into his head and he played his violin perfectly but he hasn't remembered anything specifically. Except he did think he had a grandmother in Albury with jasmine in her garden. He smelled some when we were walking."

"He does! My mother. The boys call her Nan. So he's getting better, you think?"

Tess bit at her bottom lip. "I'm not sure. He's different. He's much more uninhibited than he was before."

"In what way?"

"He was always quite reserved. All the time I've known him he was like that. Never displayed much of his emotions. Very private. Now he suddenly thinks he loves me. He never said that before and now he's saying it when he's only known me two days. As far as he knows."

"That certainly doesn't sound like David." Joyce chuckled. "Maybe it's his subconscious talking. Maybe he always wanted to tell you but wasn't game."

"Hardly." Could it be true? "He said it was a deep feeling he had, that he knows me. But we never really knew each other even as students and he didn't approve of me at all."

"You're a very pretty girl. He'd have to be blind not to notice that."

"Oh. Thank you." She smiled into the phone. If only her own mother had been like Joyce, so matter-of-fact. So caring and comfortable and easy to talk to.

"How do you feel about him, Tess, if you don't mind me asking?"

"I've always loved him and he knows that," Tess said candidly. "But if I accept that he loves me, I feel as if I'm taking advantage of him because he's not really himself. Does that sound stupid?"

"No, not at all. It sounds to me like a girl who is full of integrity. Exactly the type of girl he needs. Especially after the experience he had in America with that floozy." Joyce's voice turned hard. The same protective edge she'd used in the hospital before Doug intervened.

"A floozy?" Tess would have laughed if Joyce hadn't sounded so bitter. Some people in the orchestra would call her a floozy. Yvonne for example. The word conjured visions of peroxided hair and false eyelashes, tight-fitting skirts and too much cleavage à la 1950s starlets.

"That's exactly what she was. Marianne. And a nasty little piece of work she turned out to be."

"He hasn't mentioned her to me."

"Don't tell him I told you."

"It wouldn't matter. He won't remember her." Tess laughed, and after a moment Joyce did do.

"That's right," she said. "And with any luck he never will."

"What did she do?"

"He never said much but I gather he fell quite hard for her and she wanted to marry him—or said she did—but it turned out she'd had several men in the same situation and enjoyed playing them. She latched onto him after a magazine did one of those silly articles on eligible bachelors. He'd done a series of concert performances and was on a talk show and in the newspaper so the orchestra thought it was good publicity. He wasn't keen as you can imagine."

"It sounds very unlike the David I know. Knew," she amended sadly.

"Anyway this Marianne liked the glamor of it all—performing onstage, TV appearances, recognition in the social world and all that. Things David doesn't care about at all. Basically she was a groupie. The man who replaced David was an actor in a TV series. When all the attention shifted to the next fad and it became apparent David wasn't going to change his lifestyle or his focus for her she dumped him."

"Nice."

But so true to the man she loved. The one she understood. Where was he and would he ever come back?

Chapter Nine

Tess and David rode to the rehearsal in a taxi.

"I'll have to buy another car," she said as they sat in the backseat being swung wildly from side to side by a driver who seemed to think he was in a rally.

David grimaced. "I'm sorry. I feel terrible about that. You trusted me with your car and I smashed it up."

"I'm just glad you didn't smash yourself up."

"It was insured, wasn't it?"

"Yes but if they pay out in full I'll have to pay off the loan I took out to buy it in the first place. There won't be much left over."

"How does that work?"

"Depends what their assessor thinks, but from what the policeman said it was completely crushed by the truck. Got dragged along under the wheels. They'd never be able to repair it so they'll pay me the agreed value." Her beautiful Diva. She couldn't let him see how upset she was. It was true that in the initial shock of hearing about the accident she was simply happy to have David in one piece but as time passed the loss of the Diva sank in more and more. Her scheme had failed spectacularly. She'd never be able to pull something like it again. The Stu factor was an inescapable blockage if nothing else.

On that subject the best she could hope was that he never discovered David had been driving the Diva when he crashed. Tess' car, yes, but let Stu think he'd been in the Toyota. David would have to be carefully primed if Stu visited again. Tess sighed and clung on grimly as the taxi shot around a corner on an amber light. Would these complications never end? Dimly remembered words from a high school English class danced through her head. *"Oh what a tangled web we weave when first we practice to deceive."*

Tangled was an understatement.

David stood at the back of the rehearsal hall with Ian Moore, who Tess had introduced as the orchestral manager. It was disconcertingly obvious everyone knew him. After ten minutes of enthusiastic greetings, vigorous handshakes, slaps on the back and well-meant best wishes from total strangers he wanted to skulk away and hide in a cupboard.

Tess murmured something to Ian who promptly led him to a room with CONDUCTOR written on it in ornate gold lettering. He tapped and went in immediately, not waiting for a summons from within. "Viktor, here's David," he said to whoever was inside. Presumably the conductor.

A tall, dark, hawk-faced man put some papers on the table, smiled, and extended his hand. "I'm so glad to see you, David," he said in a richly accented voice.

"Thank you."

"I am Viktor Zakharoff, conductor of the City Symphony. We gave a magnificent concert together last week. You played the Beethoven Violin Concerto with us as your debut. You received rave reviews."

"So Tess tells me." David smiled weakly. At least this Viktor spoke calmly and coherently and didn't gush or bemoan his situation.

"Perhaps if you listen to the rehearsal some little memories will filter through." Viktor regarded him through kindly eyes, so dark they were nearly black. An imposing man. Impressive bearing. A very good musician. David frowned as the thought slipped and slid inside his mind. Viktor tilted his head enquiringly. "Something?"

"I thought . . . no. It's gone."

Viktor placed long, firm fingers on David's arm. "How frightening it must be."

David nodded. "It is, it's terrifying at times." He glanced at Ian who stood silently by, listening attentively. "But Tess has been marvelous. She's been my rock. I rely on her completely."

"Tess has a very generous, kind heart," said Ian.

"That's what I think too. What sort of relationship do I have with her? Do you know?"

Ian and Viktor exchanged glances. Embarrassed. Ian said, "Oh well. I don't know really . . . You were students together in Canberra and you've been staying at her house, paying rent as a tenant. You seem very good friends. Beyond that I couldn't say."

"I think perhaps others' perceptions can be quite misleading," said Viktor. "What does anyone know about someone else's relationships? One has to discover the true essence of a person for oneself."

"I've certainly been given that opportunity." David smiled wryly. "I have no option but to discover everyone as a fresh face. No baggage attached. Myself included."

"In some ways that could be a blessing," said Ian. "Any naughty little secrets can remain buried." He looked at his watch. "I think we should start the rehearsal, Viktor."

David followed the pair back to the rehearsal hall where a cacophony of instruments drowned any attempt at conversation. Ian indicated some chairs along the side wall and they sat while Viktor strode forward to take his place at the front on a small raised podium. The racket died down. A balding, slim man stood at the front of the violin section and nodded at the woman playing oboe. As the wind section began tuning to the note she gave, Ian said, "That's Stan. He's filling in your position until you rejoin us."

"If I ever do."

"Of course you will," said Ian. "A cousin of mine fell

off a horse once and hit his head. He spent the rest of the day wondering what he'd just been doing but he functioned perfectly well on autopilot. He had a good sleep and woke up remembering everything."

"I've had several good sleeps since the accident and woken up remembering nothing."

"You got a harder whack than he did, that's all, plus the much bigger trauma of the accident itself."

David grinned. What optimism. Wish he shared it. Viktor raised his arm and the orchestra began the first piece. "That's Debussy," he exclaimed as the first notes shimmered into the air. Beautiful, evocative. " 'L'Après-midi d'une Faune.' "

He turned to Ian who was nodding and smiling. "Yes, yes."

The orchestra was very good. He didn't need a memory to judge that. And the music was wonderful. David sat in rapt attention absorbing every note, every comment from Viktor, every tiny adjustment to dynamics, phrasing, and tempo. Fascinating.

"I should have brought my violin," he said to Ian.

"Do you think you could join in?"

"I could try. I know this piece. I must have played it many times before."

"The program for the next concert is all standard works. Favorites. The Debussy. Mozart Symphony No. 40 and the Hummel Trumpet Concerto with Mike Hauptmann, our lead trumpet."

"When's the next rehearsal?"

"Tomorrow morning."

"I'll play."

"I'll give you the music to look at this afternoon."

On the way home in another, less wildly driven taxi he said to Tess, "I feel I belong there."

"You do." She squeezed his hand.

He gripped her fingers tightly. "And I feel you belong with me."

Tess rubbed her lips together and looked out her side window.

By the following week the insurance company had agreed the Diva was a total write-off. A check would be sent. Her debt would be cleared and she'd come out with about eighteen thousand dollars. But no Diva.

"I'll have to find another car," Tess said as they prepared dinner on Friday night. "Something cheap."

"I won't be much help. I don't know anything about cars."

"Are you sure?"

"Positive. They do nothing for me. Not the way music does. As soon as the orchestra started last week I knew it was what I do. I've had no trouble playing."

"It's pretty amazing, really. That you can do your job but not remember anything."

"It's because it's an automatic function like the doctor said. Muscle memory. My eyes see it and the brain processes the notes straight to my fingers. You know what it's like; you don't have to remember how to play every time you pick up the instrument."

"No, that's true."

He stirred the tomato sauce he'd made for the lasagna after careful study of a recipe book. Tess beat an egg into a bowl of cottage cheese.

"We fit well together, don't we?" he said. "We should get married."

Tess dropped her fork onto the bench and a glob of mixture fell to the floor. "What?"

David stepped over the mess and put his arms around her. "You're an amazing woman and I love you. I know I do. You've looked after me and I don't know what I would have done without you. I need you, Tess, and I want you with me for the rest of my life."

"Your sauce is burning," she said shakily.

"I don't care if it burns." But he turned swiftly and switched off the gas. "I want an answer. Will you marry me?"

"No."

"No?" He squeezed her tighter. "Try again." She tried to look into his eyes but couldn't. If she did she'd collapse and say yes, yes, a million times yes. He nuzzled his lips across her throat, nibbling and kissing toward her mouth.

"Oh, David, I can't say yes."

"Because?" A kiss.

"Your memory."

"But you love me." More kisses, each tempting, persuading. Inviting.

"Yes." Barely audible.

"You don't want to marry anyone else."

"No." On a breath.

"Say yes."

"No." She couldn't say more. His lips prevented speech, thought, breathing. Definitely brain function. Even time stopped.

"Say you'll consider it," he murmured into her mouth.

"I'll consider it."

"Thank you. Now let me get on with my sauce, please, you wanton hussy."

Tess grinned and wiped up the glob of cottage cheese. Could this happiness last? Would life with David always be so sweet? How long did she have in this cloudland?

Paradoxically the answer was so long as he failed to remember. When the past came crashing back it was over. But she still couldn't bring herself to wholly embrace the new David. They couldn't marry for three years or she'd lose everything and if she tried to explain that reason for saying no—Daddy's will—things would become very complicated all over again.

Nothing could be resolved while he was in this twilight state. If he loved her now he should love her regardless of the past. He wouldn't forget the way he felt.

On the way home from Tai Chi the next morning Tess stopped in at the bakery for fresh croissants. A breakfast on the patio exactly like the first one they'd had might jog something loose. She'd meant to do it earlier but the weather hadn't been right. Too rainy for the last week. Today was perfect.

He was up, his shower was running. She sliced fruit and set the table with the same crockery and the same napkins as before. He appeared as she carried the teapot outside.

"Breakfast on the terrace. How perfect," he said.

"We did the this the very first day you arrived. You were so zonked from the flight you were almost comatose."

The dogs trotted around the corner of the house. At least Fid trotted, Hannibal staggered. Fid bounded up to David and licked his hand. "Morning, Fid," he said.

Hannibal paused to cast a watery eye in their direction then continued on into the house. Tess poured tea. David hadn't commented on the dogs at all. He accepted Fid and had hardly seen Hannibal.

"The dogs are usually allowed indoors," she said. "Do you mind? I've kept them out so far because of the rain but . . ."

He shrugged. "Doesn't bother me. It's your house." He forked mango and pineapple onto his plate.

"I thought I'd go car shopping today. I'll look in the paper."

"Will you get the same thing?"

Tess laughed softly. "No. I'll never be able to have one of those again. I'll find something sensible this time."

"Why wasn't it a sensible car?"

"It was a fast sports car and I loved it but it wasn't really much use in the city."

"Being sensible isn't always the best way to live."

Tess stopped with her teacup in midair, mouth open in surprise.

He smiled. "What?"

"You were the most sensible, careful, organized person I've ever met. I never thought I'd hear you say something like that. You looked down your nose at me because I was messy, disorganized, and the most irresponsible person you'd ever met."

"Impossible," he said calmly. "I haven't seen any sign of any of irresponsibility at all. Quite the opposite. Disappointingly and frustratingly so." He grinned that cheeky grin.

Tess shut her mouth and shook her head. She laughed. Now she knew how Alice felt in Wonderland. A complete shift in paradigm was very disconcerting.

David continued eating. Croissants were delicious. He must have eaten them before with jam. Couldn't remember it though. Couldn't remember sitting out here overlooking the garden in the shade of the big umbrella, table beautifully set with matching crockery. Tess had gone to a lot of trouble. She oozed style. Effortlessly classy. Everything she did entranced him.

He gave hovering, hopeful Fid a corner of the pastry. It disappeared in one gulp.

"How come you live here?" he asked.

"I inherited the house from my father. I grew up here. He died a few years ago."

"I'm sorry. Were you close?"

Tess licked mango juice from her lips slowly, seemed to be considering her reply. "I disappointed him constantly," she said. "He wanted a daughter who would be a social asset and marry well. I turned into a musician."

"A very good one. I'd count you as a great asset." David studied her. This subject was awkward for her; Tess didn't want to discuss it at all. He had so much to learn about her. Or relearn. "Do you have brothers and sisters?"

"One brother. Stuart. He lives in Melbourne. He was here for your concert. You got on very well together."

He nodded. "Ah, yes. You told me. I forgot." Tess smiled. "What about your mother?"

"She divorced Daddy years ago and lives in America. We don't see her."

"That's very sad." He instinctively knew families were important, parental love a given.

Tess shrugged. "Not really. I don't think about her at all. Can we talk about something else?"

"All right. Do you have a boyfriend?"

"Not at the moment." Aaron didn't count.

"Before?"

Tess hesitated. Was this the time to tell him about Raoul? Now when he was open and uninhibited. Interested in her. Nonjudgmental.

"I had a relationship with a man from the orchestra a

while back. He was very attractive and charming. Women loved him."

"And you did too?" He sat forward, a small frown creasing his brow. "I'm jealous."

Tess snorted softly. "Don't be. Beneath the charm and the smooth talk he was the same as all the rest. He liked my house and my money. When I said I didn't want him to move in and didn't want to marry him he got very nasty and started telling people I'd strung him along. He said terrible things about me at work." She bit at her lower lip. "I thought I loved him. I thought he was different but he was worse. He had another woman going at the same time. He was romancing us both to see who was the best bet." She picked up the teapot and peered inside. "We need more hot water."

"I'll get it." David took the teapot and went inside. Poor Tess. She was so sensitive and tenderhearted. What a jerk the guy must have been to treat her that way. To treat any woman that way. He didn't know what an absolute treasure he'd thrown aside. Greedy, callous, and selfish . . . something shifted in his memory. Did he know someone else like that? Tantalizingly close, but impossible to grasp the snippets, the impressions that swam in and out of the mists. He paused. Talking about mists . . .

A most incredible pong sat like a deathly fog over the kitchen. He filled the jug and switched it on while his mind swirled. That smell. Hannibal! It was Hannibal and his rotten insides. David inhaled and a curtain lifted in his brain. The Phantom. Revealed.

Memories poured in. He leaned against the bench as things slotted into place. This kitchen. He knew it well. He recognized everything. He'd made her buy those yellow rubber dishwashing gloves. He spun around. The house. Tess' house. There she sat, lovely in the bright clear light on the patio. Tess. His love. She turned her head and shaded her eyes to look inside.

He remembered. Everything.

The jug clicked off behind him. He remade the tea on automatic.

"Are you all right?" she called.

"Coming." He picked up the pot and strode outside.

"Thought you must have forgotten what you were doing." She giggled.

He placed the teapot on the table. "I remember." He looked down at her.

Tess' head jerked toward him. Her eyes widened and her lips parted but no words emerged.

"I remember everything."

"That's fantastic!" She clapped her hands and tears sprang to those big blue eyes and ran down her cheeks. She sprang up and flung her arms around him. His neck was wet. He held her away and gazed into her face.

"You lied to me." His voice grated harsh with the bitterness of hurt and misplaced trust. "I relied on you for everything and you lied."

Tess' smile turned to bewilderment then dismay. He thrust her from him.

"You took advantage of me in the worst way. You let

me think I was living here with you as a housemate and yet really you manipulated me into staying because of your debt and because quite understandably, you're scared of what Stuart would say." He spun away and paced across the floor, but rounded on her so suddenly she jumped. Guilty. "Were you going to fill me in, Tess? If I hadn't remembered by myself would you have told me about your scheming? How I shouldn't even be here, that it's an illegitimate arrangement? How you conned me into staying here and giving you that rent money?"

"It's not illegitimate, it's just . . . just against the terms of the will. It's a stupid clause." She groped for more words, a better defense. "Does it matter now?"

"Typical Tess! Does it matter? Of course it matters."

"But you said you love me."

It was said with such sorrow he nearly relented. The days since the accident, in Sydney, in this house with Tess, had paradoxically been the happiest of his life. Based in fairyland, a fantasy, but perfect. As fantasies are. He'd dreamed this could be forever. Their life, together. An impossible dream. Just like the other. He stared at her, seeing not Tess but Marianne. She'd been the one just out of reach a moment ago. The Raoul bookend. What blessed relief to have forgotten *her*. If only she'd stayed hidden in the mist. "I was wrong."

"I love you."

Did Tess think love conquered all? The trump card, wiping out lies and deception? He knew better. And so should she with her recent background.

"Oh sure. Some love! You lie to me and you won't even give me a straight answer when I ask you to marry me."

"I couldn't." Her voice rose as her face crumpled and the tears flowed. He resisted the urge to pull her into his arms. He mustn't do that, she was too soft and sexy. Too explosive. Too wild. Too flighty. Too sweet. Too damaging. Too much. Too everything.

He said bitterly, "And now I see why. You'll lose the house."

"That's not why at all! How could I say yes to you when you weren't yourself?"

"You couldn't say yes to me because I didn't know the situation and you'd have to tell me. Would you have told me? What a difficult choice. Me or this house."

Her eyes narrowed and she dragged in deep, heaving breaths, swiping her hands across her eyes. Anger replaced the tears. "What a choice for you. The real Tess or the one you invented. It's obvious you don't love me at all. I love you regardless, memory or not. I love you with all your faults and all your perfections. Why can't you—or anyone—love me the same way? I knew it was too good to last." Tess spun on her heel and marched into the house.

David sat at the table and poured more tea with shaking hands. His mind swirled with thoughts, memories, images, snippets of conversations, forgotten emotions. People, places. And overwhelmingly Tess. His love. His betrayer. Too much. He couldn't cope, couldn't handle the deluge of conflicting information and emotion. His head ached where the honey had hit it. Mum's honey from the hives down the back under the fig tree. Whatever happened to that big glass jar?

He jumped up and ran inside for the phone. Mum and Dad. They'd never lied to him, ever. They always remained the same, solid and dependable. He couldn't wait to hear their delighted voices.

When Mum recovered from her initial euphoria she said, "Tess must be very pleased and relieved. She's been absolutely wonderful, you know."

"She's happy, yes," he said cautiously. She *was* delighted. Her eyes had shone with relief and happiness. For him.

"Make sure you don't lose her, David. She's a treasure."

"I don't think you know enough about her to make that judgment," he said. But hadn't he used the very same words in his thoughts about her just half an hour ago?

"I don't know what that's supposed to mean but I know in a crisis a person's true nature shows through and Tess came up trumps. She lost that beautiful car thanks to you and she never blamed you, never spoke one word about it, and she must have been terribly upset."

The Diva. She did love that car. It was a magnificent machine. A pang of remorse for the shock and loss he'd caused her made him admit Mum was right. "That's true. But it was fully insured." A slim scale of armor against the guilt. Obviously Mum wasn't going to change her mind about Tess, but she had no idea what machinations her paragon had put into operation to get that car. Including duping her son.

His response seemed to mollify her because she changed tack and began exclaiming over his recovery again.

"Do you remember the accident? What happened?"

He screwed up his face, closed his eyes. "Vaguely. I remember leaving Coota, driving through the countryside thinking what a beautiful sunset and then . . . I think it was a kangaroo. Came out of nowhere. Did I hit it?"

"They thought that's what happened. There was blood on the bumper but it mustn't have been badly hurt because there was no sign of a body anywhere."

"That's terrible. The poor thing."

"Can't be helped, love. They're everywhere out here. You know that."

Fifteen minutes later David put the phone down with one thought clear in his mind. He couldn't stay in this house any longer. Talking to Mum had anchored him despite her stalwart support of Tess. He knew his course again now after a temporary foray into the emotional Bermuda Triangle centered around this most dangerous of women.

The whole thing had been a disaster from the start. He shouldn't have been seduced by the luxurious surroundings and her boundless, beautiful exuberance. He should have listened to his inner warning system. It had gone off as soon as Fid raced out the front door that morning with Tess screeching after him. Stupid, stupid, stupid. Served him right. His path was clear—he would concentrate on the job with the City and not allow himself distractions. He should have stayed one night, said thank you, and hightailed it out of there.

He went to the computer in the study and found the online accommodation listings. Anywhere would do for a couple of weeks. Tess could afford to give him his rent money back now and he'd insist she give it to him. On principle. If she recognized such a concept as a principle. He typed in the suburbs he wanted.

Tess hardly saw David during the weekend. He went out on Saturday afternoon without a word to her and didn't return until after dinner when he went straight to his room. She rode the bus miserably to Chatswood and looked at used cars. A far cry from the Diva but she test-drove an affordable late model Golf. The pearly silver finish was appealing, a private tribute to the departed grand lady, and the little car drove well and would be easy to park. Why not? As long as it got her where she wanted to go. She told the enthusiastic dealer she'd think about it.

On Sunday David told her he'd found a studio apartment and would be leaving.

"When?" she asked, keeping her voice flat. She'd half expected a decision like that. He only had two weeks left anyway.

"I can move in tomorrow."

She eyed him steadily. "I suppose you'll want a refund of two weeks rent."

He hesitated. He did expect it!

Tess smiled wryly. He wouldn't get a refund anywhere else along with no bond, no month's notice to quit. No legalities. She marched to the study, pulled her checkbook from the desk, and scribbled a check for six hundred dollars.

She steamed back to the kitchen waving the piece of paper. "Here."

He shook his head. "Keep it."

"You'll need it for your bond." Hard to keep the acid from her tone.

"I've already paid it."

"Right." Tess tore the slip of paper in half and half again. "Don't say I didn't offer."

David's jaw tightened and she thought he was going to say something cutting but he turned and went to his room.

After rehearsal on Thursday David appeared beside Tess as they were packing up. She concentrated on wiping the excess resin from the fingerboard of her viola.

"Tess, I've left a few things in the studio. Could I drop by and pick them up sometime, please?"

"When?" She laid the cloth over the instrument and closed the case.

"Whenever suits you. Are you going home now?"

She nodded.

"I'll follow you."

"How? I'm bussing." She nearly added "thanks to you" but didn't. He must've caught the inference because he grimaced slightly.

"I can give you a lift. I bought a car."

"That was quick."

"Well—" He shrugged.

He wasn't a bus person and he didn't have a convenient housemate with a Merc anymore, that's why, Tess thought. Nasty. She pushed those thoughts away. No point becoming bitter and twisted. She'd survived other disasters, this was just one more. At least this one wasn't a public shaming. This one was hers to struggle with in private.

She said, "I'm picking mine up tomorrow."

"What have you bought?"

"A Golf."

"Really? So have I."

"They're supposed to be very good."

"Yes. Sensible."

Tess stared at him. Was he joking? How could he joke? He'd just broken her heart, smashed it to smithereens. What sort of heartless monster was he?

"Coming?" He tilted his head, those gorgeous brown eyes regarded her steadily.

No sort of monster. He was David and she loved him. She followed him to a red Golf parked in the lot at the back of the hall.

"Didn't think you'd choose red."

"Why not?"

"Bit wild for you, isn't it?"

"It's a very good secondhand car, Tess. I didn't have any choice." He looked across at her. "But I like it. It's a safe, eye-catching color."

Of course. Safety first with David. He merged into the traffic carefully.

"Best to get into the middle lane," she said.

"Right."

"Then after the next intersection change to the left lane."

"Right."

"Sorry." No more talking. They weren't friends any more. What were they? Acquaintances? What did you call people who'd been close but now weren't? Exes? Uncomfortable, that's what you called them. The Golf was a nice little car. Hers would be similar. Henry. Compact, efficient, and sensible. Hers was definitely a Henry.

He swung into the driveway and pulled on the brake. Tess got out and removed her viola from the backseat. David collected his violin.

"I don't like leaving it in the car," he said as they walked up the path to the door. He didn't need to explain. His violin would be worth a fortune. No musician left their instrument unattended if humanly possible. "You know, I didn't even leave it in the Diva after the accident. I instinctively took it with me. Just as well."

"Just as well you got out yourself." Tess unlocked the door and deactivated the alarm. He was talking a mighty lot. For him.

He closed the door behind them. "Tess." She turned. "I'm really sorry about the Diva. Truly sorry." His brow was creased and his expression full of concern. What did he want? Forgiveness?

Tess licked her lips. She nodded. "I know." She half turned but he went on.

"It must have been terrible for you—I didn't even re-member it. I had no idea what it was you'd lost—what sort of car—the value. Mum told me you never said a word about it."

"I was only concerned for you." She met his gaze. "Hard as you find it to believe me. I really didn't care. I discovered at that moment I didn't care about the car at all."

"But you do now," he said softly.

"It's—it's a nuisance. Having to buy another one and all that." She turned and continued down the hall to the study. He followed. "But it's solved a few problems."

"Stuart."

"Yes." She put her viola down on the settee and faced him. He put his violin down against the wall.

"Have you told him?"

"About the crash?"

"No."

His smile flicked on and off and she had the feeling she'd failed another test of some sort. The kind of test she never knew she'd been taking until she failed. What was he doing here? Why quiz her about things that were no longer his concern?

"You know," she said fiercely. "You and Daddy and Stuart are all the same. You treat me like a child. Why do you do that?"

"Maybe because you act like a child a lot of the time."

"You never give me a chance! You all assume I can't do anything. You all have these massive expectations I can't fulfill because half the time I don't know what they are."

"That's ridiculous, Tess."

Such supercilious exasperation! Her blood boiled, overflowed in a torrent of anger aimed at David but fuelled by memories of a lifetime of similar dismissals.

"It's not," she yelled. "Daddy expected me to be a dutiful little girl and do exactly what he wanted me to do, which was not hang out with my friends or go shopping, go to parties, stuff that all kids do. I was supposed to stay home and study. That's why I practiced so much. I liked that and he couldn't argue it was a waste of time if he was paying for lessons. He still thought it wasn't a serious pursuit though. He wanted me to take math and economics and all those boring subjects at school and I was hopeless at them. I wanted to do Music and English and French. He said that doing arts was a waste of a good brain. Then after a while he decided I didn't have much of a brain after all."

"So instead of behaving rationally and proving him

wrong you went out and partied and got married at eighteen. Very mature." His voice, infuriatingly, barely rose a notch.

"Just because I was a bit crazy as a teenager and I sometimes still do stupid things doesn't mean I'm incompetent. I worked really hard at music and I still do. I love it."

"I know that. You're a very good musician."

Tess glared at him, her rage off the boil at the praise but simmering gently. "Stuart doesn't think so though, does he? He doesn't think this is a real job. Not like his. And it confirms his opinion of me as a hopeless, irresponsible twit."

"And if he knew what you've been up to all his suspicions would be proven."

"Just like yours."

"I don't care what you did when you were a kid, Tess. But you can hardly deny the idiocy of your recent actions. And you can't blame me for wanting nothing whatsoever to do with any of it."

"You've made your opinion very clear, thank you."

He sighed. "Look, I didn't come here to have a fight."

Poor David. Such a pain having to deal with an irrational, over emotional female. "Why did you come?" Good question, come to think of it. Why exactly? Especially if he didn't want anything to do with her as he so strongly insisted. "It sounds to me as though you came here to pick at me some more."

"To collect some music."

"I could've brought it in." She folded her arms.

"I wasn't sure exactly what was here—just let me go and get it."

"Help yourself."

Tess brushed past him and went to her room. She washed her hands and face and leaned on the basin to regroup. Why couldn't he stay away? He was carrying on as if they'd had a minor disagreement and now all was well again. Didn't he get it? She couldn't be that sort of friend anymore, not after what he'd offered and so coldly withdrew. He might be able to switch his love on and off but she couldn't. She was stuck with hers.

She went to the kitchen and filled the jug. What would it take to change his opinion of her. Prove she was worthy of loving?

David came back in through the laundry room talking to Fid and with some music in his hand.

"I miss this little guy." Fid scampered across for a pat from her then returned to look up hopefully at David.

"You said you didn't like dogs."

"Fid changed my mind. He wants his walk. Haven't you taken him yet?"

Fid bounced up and down in excitement at hearing the magic word. Tess gritted her teeth. "No."

"I'll take him." Pause. "If you don't mind?"

"Fine." She turned her back and continued to make herself coffee.

When they returned Tess was studying the paperwork associated with her new car. David came in through the laundry room whistling a theme from the trumpet concerto they'd been rehearsing.

"There's a For Sale sign on that two-story house on the corner," he said. "That's new."

Tess looked around, incredulous. So casual, as if he still lived here. He didn't. "I know."

"Bet that goes for a packet."

"Yes." She collected the papers together.

"I'll be off," he said when she didn't make any conversational offering. How could she? He was torturing her. Did he know that?

"Good-bye."

"See you tomorrow."

"Yes." She sat, waiting for him to go.

"Right. Bye." He headed for the study and emerged with his violin. Tess returned to her papers. The front door clicked shut. A few moments later the Golf's engine burst to life. Tess exhaled and sagged back in the chair.

She got up and went to the study to file the registration and insurance stuff under H for Henry in the file cabinet. The dogs would be ready for dinner so she opened cans and went to the back door.

David had left the music he'd come to collect on the washing machine.

Chapter Ten

Deliberate? Was this the old "leave an item to create a reason to return" ploy?

Why would he do that? Tess fed the dogs, her mind twisting and turning this new information, studying it from all angles. Was he having second thoughts? No doubt his new flat was a hovel compared to her place. Was this a sneaky way of edging his way back in to the Lavender Room? As a friend? Was he the same as Aaron?

Or was he sorry he'd treated her so cavalierly? Had his love survived after all? In that case why not simply say so? Grovel at her feet. She'd go and live in a hovel with him if he asked. He knew how she felt; she'd told him often enough.

Whatever the reason he couldn't come around here again. Not like today. She couldn't stand it, being toyed with. He'd broken things off, he had to reinstate them. Unequivocally. Until then . . . she'd stay away.

He had made one valid point, though. One that had crossed her own mind in the last week. To draw a line under the idiot period of her life she had to come clean to her brother. Confess all. Then she could continue into the future with a clear, sparkling conscience. No more tangles of her own making. Act like an adult. Own up.

After dinner she phoned Stuart.

"Hello, Tessie. How are you? I was thinking of giving you a call myself."

"I'm fine. Stu, do you have time to talk?"

"Yes." His voice changed instantly. Suspicious. Cautious. "What've you done?" Resigned.

Tess told him the truth about everything—the Diva, her living arrangement with David.

"I thought that whole setup was weird," he exclaimed after a moment's silence at the end of her torrent of words. "Who'd give you a convertible Merc?"

"No one," she agreed dismally.

"So David's all right now?"

"Yes."

"Thank goodness for that. I really like him, Tess. He's a good bloke."

"Yes. He likes you too."

"I'll give him a call sometime."

"Stu where does that leave me in regard to the will?"

"We-e-e-ell." Air hissed through his teeth. "I guess

technically you've broken the terms but as I'm executor I can overlook it as a minor infringement. As long as you don't have a boarder there again."

"I don't need to now. I've discharged the loan."

"Where's David living?"

"Somewhere in Artarmon."

"I thought he wanted to be near a beach."

"Yes, but he was so angry he just wanted to get away from me."

"Aaah."

"What do you mean 'aaah'?"

"You didn't tell him everything just like you still haven't told me everything, have you? Old habits die hard, Tessie. Spit it out. All of it."

"I did tell you everything." Except the humiliating bit about loving David, being loved and being dumped. Again.

"Why was he so angry then? He seemed happy enough when I was there."

"Because he hates doing anything the least bit dishonest or sneaky. He was furious that I conned him into paying rent without telling him about the will. And that I made him promise not to tell you about it when you were here."

"I can understand that."

"I'm sorry."

"I bet you are. That was a fantastic car."

"I'll never be able to afford another one."

"You will when you're thirty-five."

"Will I?"

"Tessie, you only have a few years to wait, you're thirty-two already. Have you any idea how much you'll inherit?"

"Not really." How could she? No one told her anything.

"Let's just say it'll be a great deal thanks to my brilliant investments on your behalf."

"Thank you. Fat lot of good it does me though. Like living here. I love it but it's becoming a millstone. I never know whether guys like me for me or my address and my apparent wealth. Which at the moment is nonexistent."

"David's the sort of bloke who doesn't care about any of that." His tone implied David was of an interesting species, not very familiar to Stu. He wouldn't be. Stu's friends and acquaintances read the stock market reports and understood the implications of every fluctuation in the world economy.

"I'm not so sure. He was around this afternoon saying he'd forgotten some things but I bet he hates that dump he's living in already and wants to come back here."

"Maybe he wants to see you."

"He wants nothing more to do with me. He made that very plain."

"Tess, he's pretty attracted to you. Anyone could see that."

"Not enough. Or rather, not anymore."

"Maybe he's slower off the mark than we Fullers.

I don't let a desirable girl slip by. He's not as experienced in that department, I'd say." He laughed.

"He's had a few bad experiences. There was someone called Marianne in the States who dumped him and then there was me. Untrustworthy and unreliable, that's me."

"Sounds like he can't keep away though."

"Stu," she cried. "I don't want him hanging around all the time. I'd rather not see him at all except at work. I can't stand it."

"Oh, I see. Want me to fill him in?"

"No! He knows my position." Stu the Matchmaker? He'd treat this like any other business deal. A merger. Present a report.

"Poor Tessie. Sounds like you need a holiday."

"We don't have any breaks until Christmas."

"Hang in there then."

"I'm trying to."

"Call me anytime."

"Thanks, Stu."

"And Tess?"

"Yes?"

"I never thought I'd hear you voluntarily confess to something silly you've done and you've done plenty over the years."

"I know. David said I acted like a child."

"You just acted like an adult for about the first time ever."

"Thanks. Bye."

Tess disconnected to the awareness tears were running down her cheeks. And also another surprising fact emerged along with the relief and the feeling of liberation—Stuart hadn't been angry. He'd actually been supportive. And that was another first.

Tess took David's forgotten music to the next rehearsal and placed it on his music stand before he took his seat. She chatted to Matt while they warmed up, watching furtively for David to appear. He walked in with Stan and they sat down. David looked across quickly at her. "Thanks," he called.

She nodded in response. That was that. Mike wandered in with his trumpet and began tootling bits of the Hummel. Then Viktor appeared and they were away.

During the break David caught her before she had a chance to escape from her seat.

"Thanks for bringing this in," he said. "I couldn't believe I'd left it behind."

Tess smiled politely. She stood up.

"Have you picked up the Golf yet?"

"No. I'm going after rehearsal."

"I'll drop you if you'd like."

Tess glanced around. Tim was the only person in the room, in the far corner tapping on the tympani, tuning them with his head bent close to the skins. Everyone else had charged out to grab tea and biscuits before the best ones were all gone.

"David, why are you doing this?" she hissed.

"Doing what? Offering you a lift?"

"Hanging around me all the time. Can't you see . . ." She stopped, biting her lips firmly.

"Sorry." Now he looked plain bewildered.

"You said you didn't want anything to do with me. Fine. I accept that. But if that's how you feel then leave me alone. Please."

"I thought we could be friends, at least."

A couple of flute players strolled in chattering loudly.

"No, we can't." Tess pushed past him, put her viola in its case on the bench along the rear wall, and almost ran from the room.

But he was waiting for her when they finished. Tess tried to avoid him but short of making a scene it was impossible. She'd given the orchestra enough to gossip about. Never again. Everyone was used to seeing them coming and going together. They were unremarkable.

He steered her to the Golf and she allowed herself to be packed in. He placed her viola and his violin in the rear hatch.

"Where are we going?" he asked.

"Chatswood. Railway Street."

He swung out onto the road. Tess sat in silence. He drove in silence. What was the deal here?

"I owe you a few lifts," he said eventually.

"You actually owe me a whole car."

He grimaced. "I suppose I do."

May as well rub it in. "Stu said I'll be able to buy another one when I turn thirty-five. And that's only a few years away now. I inherit a packet. Megabucks, according to Stu."

"Really?" His eyes opened wide. He pulled an impressed face.

"Daddy was *very* rich." She turned her head slightly and gave him the Fuller look.

He didn't react. Railway Street was next on the right. David slipped round the intersection on the amber arrow.

"It's there on the left." He pulled into the gutter.

Tess opened the door. "Thanks."

He said, "See you." She closed the door but before she could open the rear hatch to retrieve her viola he'd pulled out into the traffic.

"I don't believe it!" She stared after the red hatchback in amazement. Had he done that deliberately? Maybe her petty little jabs had hit home despite his lack of response and he'd been so furious he couldn't wait to get her out of the car. She was darned if she'd phone him. At least the viola was in safe hands.

Tess turned on her heel and went in to claim Henry, who was waiting, polished and gleaming, in front of the office. Cute but no Diva. But did she want another Diva? She'd rather have David.

He arrived later that afternoon, standing on the doorstep with the viola case in his hand. She took it without a word, body rigid, fingers clammy, and backed inside.

"Tess." She held the door half closed against the attraction, the absolute, overwhelming passion she had for this man who no longer loved her and seemed intent on tormenting her. "Can I come in?"

She shook her head, unable to speak. All the words were gone, all used up. He didn't understand anything she said. Or ignored it. She hadn't thought of him as cruel.

"Please?"

"No." It came out hoarse and unrecognizable.

"I'll say it here then." He licked his lips but his eyes never left hers. "Tess, I can't leave you alone. I tried. I couldn't—can't. It took me about a day to realize how hopeless that was. I know you want me to go away and stay away. I don't blame you."

Fid came pattering down the hall, his paws clicking and scraping. He spied David and dashed through the gap.

"Ooh, Fid!" Tess put the viola down and let the door go in an effort to catch him. David stepped inside quickly.

"Come," he said sternly. Fid darted after him squirming and grinning.

Tess shut the door. He hadn't moved farther into the house; he waited close to her in the hallway.

"So," he said.

"So what?" Tess looked up into his face. He stared into her eyes. Searching, intense. She armed herself, attacked because she had no defense when he looked at her that way. "What are you saying? You want to come back and live here with me again? Is that it? You've discovered that your new flat is too small and poky and uncomfortable and you're regretting that rash decision to leave? You can't come back. Stu said he'd overlook what happened but . . ."

David touched a finger to her lips so gently she closed her eyes tight to steel herself against him. He flowed over her. He covered her, enveloped her, swamped her. How could he do this? His finger left her lips.

He said, "The days after I lost my memory were the happiest days I've ever spent in my entire life. I didn't know it at the time, of course, because I couldn't remember my life. But afterward, after I left, I saw clearly what had happened. I'd allowed myself to be free, to love you the way I wanted to. And I wanted that for the rest of my life. Everything else seemed worthless and gray by comparison. I love you, Tess. I shouldn't have doubted you, I should—I do—love you as you are. I'm sorry."

Tess' eyes opened slowly. He was still staring at her but his expression was one of hope. Vulnerable. Exposed. Doubting. Wondering if he'd lost her love.

"I couldn't believe how happy I was then too," she whispered. "I kept thinking it was a dream. I've loved you for so long—but I didn't think you'd ever love me.

You never took me seriously." She edged forward and rested her cheek on his chest, slid her arms around his waist. She sighed. "I knew when you remembered you'd be mad at me again."

His arms were around her now. Comforting. Strong. "But you still tried to help me regain my memory."

"Of course. We had to try."

"We," he murmured.

"Yes, we."

She turned her face up for his kiss and the world slid away.

"Will you move back in with me?" she whispered after some time.

He frowned. "We can't, can we? Quite honestly I don't care where we live as long as we're together."

"Neither do I, in which case we should stay here rather than your little place."

"How? Don't you lose the house if you marry before you're thirty-five?"

"Are you proposing?"

He laughed and kissed her again. "I suppose I am. Again."

"Stu has to give his approval for me to marry. He likes you. He'll approve. Stupid to leave a place like this and rent something like what we looked at. Don't you think?"

David studied her with raised eyebrows.

"And we have two dogs, don't forget," she added. "Makes it very difficult. Also, Hannibal at close quarters would be . . . ummm . . ." She grinned.

"Life-threatening," he supplied. "So you don't want to move."

"No. Do you?"

"No." He dropped a kiss on her mouth. "So there is such a thing as having your cake and eating it too."

"Stick with me and I'll show you how it's done."